DIARY OF A MASQUERADE

M. QUEENI GREEN

DEDICATION

This book is dedicated to YOU for taking the steps
needed to stop preying, and start praying.
I applaud you for removing the mask,
and allowing God to FREE the real you.
You shall recover it all!

INTRODUCTION

"Diary of A Desperate Mind" left readers on edge, and had them asking questions: What happened to the Postman? How did Makayla's life turn out? and more... Dive inside this new *Diary* and you may find the answers to your impending questions.

Diary of A Masquerade expounds on the character Chastity. Take an intimate look inside her life, her thoughts, and her road to unveil, and prevail. Does she win, lose, or draw?

PLEASE NOTE:
Italicized text – are diary entries
Non – Italicized text – are real time events

The views, opinions, and language expressed in this book by the characters are NOT supported by the author. They are only used for literary content and authentication of the characters. We apologize in advance if anyone is offended.

<u>REVIEW</u>

Diary of a Masquerade invites the reader to THINK about the never ending "Masquerade Ball" trauma creates. Dancing with Chastity the reader discovers how much she has invested in creating an identity shaped by her trauma. No longer able to groove to the dramatic beat at the "Masquerade Ball" called LIFE, Chastity unmasks how unchecked trauma causes the prey to become the predator. Unveiling how masks make shallow what God has intended to be deep—causes Chastity to stop spinning out of control. If you have every been tired of spinning around at the "Masquerade Ball" called LIFE, this book is for you!

Dr. Angelita Clifton

ACKNOWLEDGMENTS

The Epiphany is, I'm fulfilling my destiny, and leaving a legacy for my family. Lord I thank you for divine revelation. Lord, I thank you for my family who understands this life is not my own. I make room for you to do what you want to do in and through me, I just want to do your will.

To Dr. Angelita Clifton, words cannot express how much I appreciate you, admire you, and thank God for you. You are an inspiration, and a HUGE blessing to me, and the body of Christ. I'm honored to be your "honorary" baby sister and friend. I was almost gas lit.. but I got out!!!

To my husband, THANK YOU for loving me as only YOU can.
For covering me, praying with me, and waring in the spiritual realm for me.
It's you and me for life babe. You always give me space, let me sleep late and you always figure it out so I can get it all done.
I love you more and more every day.

Table of Contents

M. QUEENI GREEN

THE BREAKDOWN

"Hey Sister…. So good to see you. It seems like these moments are getting further apart, and fewer each year. How are you and the family doing?" Mikayla extends her arms and gives Chastity a long warm embrace. As she takes her seat, she replies, "Girl, I'm tired, those twins are giving me a run for my money! Other than that, we are good. God is faithful and kind. How are you and your family doing?" The waiter interjects, "What can I get you beautiful young ladies today?" Chastity quickly says, "Well, since you put it that way, I'll take an Ultimate Pina Colada, and she'll take a Raspberry Lemon Breeze." Mikayla chuckles and adds, "She got it right, and can you bring us those jerk wings too. Hmmm - they are so delicious." Chastity nods in agreement as she closes the menu and places it on the table. She focuses in on Mikayla and asks, "What's new in your life? Certainly, there must be some new and exciting things going on in your life." "No, nothing new with me." Mikayla replies, while never lifting her head from the menu. "Well, there's a lot going on with me. I don't even know where to begin." Chastity sighs and picks up the menu. She continues, "Lee and I have been fighting like cats and dogs. He's not happy in this marriage, and I'm afraid that one day I'll come home and he's gone." "Well, first of all is it physical or verbal?" Mikayla interjects. Chastity smiles and proclaims, "Verbal, just verbal - he's not abusive at all. You know he's a God-fearing man, and girl - I've never heard him cuss." Mikayla asks, "So, what is all the fighting about?" "He sat me down yesterday and said, Chastity, I'm serious we need counseling or this marriage isn't going to make it." in a deep voice as if Lee was talking, then Chastity laughed. Mikayla places her straw in her drink, and swirls it around while asking Chastity, "What do you think? Do the two of you need counseling or do YOU need counseling?" Chastity became very defensive and responded, "What kind of question in that? You've known me since college, through marriages, divorce, death, births of three of my children, come on now - what kind of question is that? You know damn well I don't need counseling. I've always been strong. I've always held it down, and kept it moving. You know I'm about my business and my family, and frankly I'm offended that you even said that. Mikayla waiting patiently for Chastity to finish her rant and as she takes a sip of her drink she jumps in and says, "It is not my intent to offend you. You're right, I have known you seems like forever. I feel that we are closer than sisters, and I believe we can have an honest conversation with each other." "We can and we are." Chastity says while she's still talking. Mikayla says, "Let me finish for once. That's what I'm talking about. You do need counseling Chastity. The world does not evolve around you. You hide behind your business, your babies, your husband, your house, your lavish vacations, and whatever else you can think of to hide what's really missing on the inside. Your brokenness, your hurt, your grief, your disappointments, and even your past. Yes, you keep it moving because you never take time to deal or heal from anything before you're on to the next thing to get your mind off the last thing that went wrong. I love you, I want you to be happy, but you got some demons that you need to deal with so you can be healed and delivered. When are you going to admit it, and address it. You can't keep running and hiding forever. You're always plotting and scheming, and looking for ways to take advantage of a situation, and when things don't go your way you pounce on people like a savaged wolf. That tongue of yours devours people verbally and you're physically abusive. It's time Chastity, it's time... Lee is partially right, counseling is needed, but it's you that needs the counseling." She picks up a chicken wing in one hand and her napkin in another and Chastity knocks the wing out her hand and says, "How dare you little girl...how dare you think that you can speak to me like that. Whose side are you on? We'll always be family, and don't you ever forget that. Lee and his counseling suggestion can go straight to hell for all I care. I am hurt that you would say those things to me and I will not stay here and break bread with Mrs. Perfect. You think you got it all together, but always remember I was there when you were desperate for a man, desperate for love, so desperate in the mind that you almost married Gay Jay. So, don't you ever get it twisted with me again. Enjoy your lunch punk, because if we were in private that chicken isn't all that I would knock out of you." Then she slams a $100 bill on the table, gather's her things, and storms off leaving Mikayla in the restaurant in tears. Mikayla shouts out to her over her shoulder, "You're a vessel for the devil and I'm praying for you."

Dear Diary,

Today was a day that I will never forget as long as I live. I never thought that Mikayla and I would ever not be friends. Today she said some things to me that hurt me to my core. Honestly, I don't understand how the argument even got to where it ended.

After me and my first husband split I decided to go back to college, and get my Master's Degree. Mikayla answered my ad for a roommate and she's been one of my closest friends ever since. She is the little sister I never had. We spent almost every holiday, and summer together when we lived together. We had no desire to go home. She was raised by her grandparents, and although they were still living, she didn't want to go home out of fear that she would run into her ex, "Mr. You Know Who." We always laughed about her vow to never say his name again, and now they are married and have twins.

Mikayla is the God-mother to all my children, even Lexon, who was 18 months old when she met him. She has been there for me, and I for her. I am so broken by her words today - they cut deep into my soul.

One minute we were discussing what I don't even remember, the next thing I knew Mikayla called me a vessel for the devil... and she's is praying for my deliverance. I am still speechless. The best thing I did, was gather my things and leave, or it may have ended really bad for her.

I am still trying to process how the conversation moved from where it started to where it ended. This is too much right now.

"Good Evening Mrs..." "What's so damn good about it?" Chastity cuts off Consuela. Lee says, "Come on Babe. That's not right. Please, not again tonight. How was your lunch with Mikayla, she always puts you in a good head space?" "Well since you asked" Chastity snaps at Lee and proceeds to share with him what happened over lunch. Lee listens and then says, "I think she's right, counseling by yourself would be an opportunity for you to work through some things that happened before us? Chastity looked through Lee and said in an eerily calm and emotionless voice, "Maybe I will. Maybe I am crazy. Maybe it will keep me from killing all of you for thinking you know better than I do what's best for me." Then she walks out the kitchen.

Dear Diary,

My heart is still aching from yesterday's blow out with Mikayla. I tried to talk to Lee about it, but he agrees with her. He said that I am void of emotions, and that I go through life operating in rigid routines that cannot be injected with spontaneity or emergencies. Lee ended our conversation with, "You need professional help."

Why is everyone jumping on me? I have carefully calculated systems that work to keep me balanced and on task. No, I don't like interruptions, I've had too many in my life that I couldn't control, but now I'm in control and I don't want to let go.

This diary is the only place I can share what's going on deep inside me. I know I don't share in tears, and that's because I have none left. Life has not been kind to me, and there are moments I still hold inside, things I haven't shared even here.

Maybe I do need counseling. I don't know. I'll sleep on it.

Dear Diary,

After many arguments with Lee, and now Mikayla, today I reluctantly met with a therapist. I paced in the rain for almost thirty minutes before my 9:00 AM appointment. There were moments I wanted to just leave. I was arguing with the inner me to stay because I want to be better for my husband and children. Just when I made up my mind to finally walk away a cherry red Mercedes Benz coup whipped in the driveway. A tall slender woman popped out and quickly opened up her umbrella, extending apologies for her tardiness; citing that there was a terrible accident, and traffic was detoured causing her delay. She quickly opened up the door, and extended her hand for me to enter first. I said thank you, and walked in. To my left were book cases eloquently decorated and coordinated by color with books and accessories. Clearly, she doesn't read the books, they are only there for display only.

Sitting in front of the bookshelves was a beautiful mahogany desk with intricate carvings, and a white leather tufted nail head office chair, and cherry hardwood floors shine between an exotic area rug. To my right was two nail head trim tufted back leather chairs, a chaise-lounger in an ultra-suede, and a comfy leather couch filled with pillows. The colors were all very serene in relaxing shades of soft greens, browns, burnt orange, and off white. I must admit I immediately felt relaxed.

I sat on the comfortable couch, and cocooned myself in the pillows. I continued to look around and take in the décor: the glass tables, abstract wall art, degrees from Yale, and Harvard. She asked from the far-left corner of the office, "Would you like something to drink? Tea, coffee, water, or juice?" I requested, "a cup of tea." She said, "Coming right up!" A few moments later she emerged from the corner with tea for two. I thought to myself… I am going to like her.

She placed the tray down on the table between us, and took a seat in one of the tufted leather chairs and said, "Tell me about yourself. Why are you here on this God-awful rainy day?" We both laughed. Then out of nowhere, I just began to cry. Not one of those "pretty cries." I begin to sob inconsolably. The water hose was on full blast with snot running from my nose and everything. I could feel her taking the tea cup from my hand, and replacing it with a box of tissues. Then she gently holds my other hand, and says," It's ok, let it out. You are safe here." I was trying to get myself together, yet I sensed that I needed to get it out. I felt like I had been holding it in for too long. Thirty years too long. I haven't cried in thirty years, not one tear, not even at my mother's funeral. Imagine that, who doesn't cry at their mother's funeral? I whaled louder and louder, and she gently laid me down on the pillows, and said, "It's alright. You're safe now." After about thirty minutes, I finally was able to pull myself together and I told her that I'm emotionally empty, and it's causing huge problems in my marriage and friendships. My husband wants us to go to marriage counseling, but I insisted that I come alone, first, because there are some things about me he doesn't know, second, because there are things I don't want him to know.

I met my current husband Lee, as I was leaving the court house after my ex-lover, Dwayne was sentenced for vehicular manslaughter for killing my second husband, Ezekiel. Dwayne and I became lovers six months after I got married. There was nothing wrong in my marriage, and I loved my husband: Dwayne just happened. Dwayne and I were very compatible; and, he listened and followed directions very well. Dwayne was tall, honey brown, his body was chiseled to perfection. He was former military, turned mail carrier. He was obedient, and strong. The perfect muse. I purchased a wedding band for him to symbolize our "chamber marriage." I remember the day I gave it to him, he was so excited, he surrendered to me for hours.

I didn't know him as a person, and never cared to get to know him. He was simply in my life to fulfill my injurious desires, and he messed everything up by falling in love with me. I called the Postmaster and had his route changed to one of my girlfriend's neighborhood, and in hopes that in her desperation that she would take him off my hands. But because he wore that damn ring every day, she would slam the door in his face... every day. Dang Mikayla, why couldn't you look past the ring, ask a question - he wasn't married.

Anyway, Dwayne came to my house to profess his love to me and, to confront my husband. He met a side of me... he wasn't ready to meet. I grabbed the leather braided whip that was hanging on the wall, and I began swinging. I was yelling at him to leave, to get out of my house. How dare he come there, and think he was going to ruin my home, my marriage!?! I chased him out the door, and beat him like a slave all the way to his car. He sped off out of my driveway, and when he got to the end of my block he didn't stop, and the next thing I heard was this awful crash that halted my breath, and my heart at the same time. I remember Consuela, my maid, taking the whip from my hand, and leading me in the house saying, "Mrs. Chastity, this has to stop. You need help." Deep inside I knew she was right. But, I also felt that that sound I heard had changed my life forever, and it certainly did. A few minutes later my neighbor called and said, "Chastity, you need to come up the block, your husband has been in an accident."

I grabbed my keys, but I don't know why because, I ran up to the entrance of our development, and there I witnessed the most horrific scene: Cops, ambulances, fire trucks, people everywhere. Dwayne was talking to one of the police officers. He was pointing, shaking his head, and rubbing his hands across his forehead in disbelief. In the center of the street was my husband's motorcycle, mangled, and pieces everywhere. His body was laying lifeless, partially on the curb, and in the street. I looked down and near my feet was his helmet, I saw his face, and he was looking at me. I bent down and reached out to pick it up, and a police officer stopped me, and yelled, "You can't touch that ma'am." I said, "It's my husband's helmet." He slowly walks me over to a female officer for consolation, but I am not crying. I am taking in everything that is going on around me. My neighbors, Patty and Marie, are crying and hugging each other. I saw more of my neighbors coming to the scene while walking their children, and pets. The emergency personnel were running back and forth, the police securing the scene, and there are people all around me crying, and I am just standing there, emotionless. The police lady said to me, "Ma'am are you alright?" I responded, "No." I was in shock and disbelief.

All I could think about was that my two worlds had just collided, and exploded right in front of me. My husband is dead, and my lover killed him. They never met, never laid eyes on each other. Dwayne and Ezekiel would not know each other if they ran into each other at the grocery store. Yet, one just killed the other. I was perplexed as to how this could have happened? It's my fault, I just chased him from my house. But, I had no idea that my husband was on his way home. How did this happen? Why did this to happen? Why didn't I end things with Dwayne a year ago when he told me that he was in love with me?" All these thoughts were racing through my mind at the same time, yet I was void of feelings, tears, emotions in that moment of distress. I was physically present yet, I was emotionally absent, and I have been this way since a child.

The therapist jolted me from that scene and said, "That's our time for today." While looking down at her planner she continued her conversation and gave me another appointment.

On my way home I couldn't help but wonder, what does she think about me? Does she think I'm crazy? I guess I'll find out soon enough.

Dear Diary,
It's time to take an honest look at who I am, and why I'm the way I am. I'll start from the beginning: I grew up in Detroit, in a dysfunctional household. My Momma was a functional addict, abusing drugs, and alcohol. I have never known, or heard

mention of who my Dad is. I'm an only child. I grew up in the house with my Grandmother, my Uncle Elroy, Uncle Ray, Uncle Reece, and Aunt Rita. My Momma said that she basically dropped out of school to raise them and me, but my Grandmother says that she was a liar, a drunk, and a drug addict. My Momma was hit by a car, and killed on my 18th birthday. Her addiction consumed her, and ultimately took her from me way too soon.

My aunts, and uncles have all battled addiction, at one point or another in their lives, and they all blamed my Momma for their addiction. My Grandmother, and all of my Momma's siblings have always treated me as an outcast because I have never used drugs, or drank alcohol. My Momma always told me that if she ever caught me using any kind of drugs, even aspirin, she would kill me herself. She was not going to let the streets kill me since they already had her, and that was enough in this family.

My Momma was functional; she worked, and made sure I went to school. She told me since I was a little girl, that I had to go to college. She encouraged me to move far away from Detroit, to never come back, and to create a new identity for myself. She wanted me to leave all the bad stuff behind, and only remember the good. She even told me that it was acceptable to forget her, if she was a part of my pain.

My Momma had a lot of boyfriends, and there was much violence in our home. There were so many things that happened to me. I believe; my Momma knew about those things. Yet, we never spoke about them, even things we both knew weren't right. The secrets of our household have never been spoken or written about — EVER... We always got up the next day, put on our best faces, and acted as if nothing ever happened. It was weird, and normal all at the same time.

I believe this is where I learned not to address problems and situations. Just be strong, put on your face on, and keep it moving.

Ring, ring, "Hello, this is your Aunt Rita, I'm calling to tell you that your Grandmother passed away on yesterday. The funeral will be on next Saturday, but you need to be here by Thursday for the reading of the will. Hello, are you still there?" "Yes, Aunt Rita, I will be there. Do you need me to do anything for the funeral? Chastity responded. "No, my Momma had her affairs in order, and everything is taken care of. Just make sure you get here by Thursday, you hear? It's important business we need to take care of for her estate. Alright? I love you, Bye now." Chastity hangs up the phone, sends a text to Lee and Mikayla advising them of her Grandmothers passing, what she has to do, and returns to work as if she never received the call.

Dear Diary,

Well, I guess I am really going to get to the heart of the matters of my life. I have to go back to Detroit because my Grandmother passed away.

One of the things that made my friendship with Mikayla so strong is that we both hated going home; we become each other's family.

I'm going back to Detroit, but I will not take my family with me. This is something I need to do on my own. Grandma always said, "Everything happens according to

Gods divine will and timing." I guess this is one of those times. Oh well, I embrace it, and accept it.

It's   time   to   face   ME!

A TRIP DOWN MEMORY LANE

Dear Diary,

I am about to board the plane back to Detroit. I am anxious, nervous, and excited all at the same time. I am anxious - to face ME, nervous - about what I may find, and excited - to get it over with. I need closure.

Dear Diary,

I made it safely to Detroit. I decided to ride through town in the rental, and visit some of my old hang outs. I remember Mr. Ron used to watch me all the time. He would follow me home from school, and watch me while I hung out with my friends after school.

One evening as I was walking home, he came out of nowhere offering me a ride. He was polite, so I accepted. Along the way he told me that if I ever needed anything all I had to do was ask, and he would make sure I got it. He was always very kind to me.

DIARY OF A MASQUERADE

When I was turning twelve all I wanted for my birthday was a pair of roller skates, which my mother refused to buy; out of fear that I would fall and break my neck. That was the first time I asked Mr. Ron for anything, and he got them for me. Oh, the joy I felt when I opened the box. I unwrapped the box with care because the paper was so beautiful. They were the exact pair I wanted; all white with neon pink wheels that glow in the dark, and I was so excited. I remember him whispering in my ear, "I did something for you, now you need to do something for me." The feeling in the pit of my stomach, when I think about it, the look in his eyes as he winked at me, and his side grin showing his gold tooth. But in my excitement, I quickly smiled back and said, "Anything for you, Mr. Ron."

One night a few weeks later, I went roller skating with my friends. When we came out the rink, there was Mr. Ron, waiting. He was polite as always, and he offered to give us all a ride home. After he dropped all my friends off, he drove me to his house. He lived on the other side of town, in a big house, on a big piece of property. He pulled way in the back of his property, which had a big pond. It was beautiful. He came around to my side of the car, and opened the door for me. He held his hand out to me, and helped me out the car. He said to me, "This is how a lady should to be treated." He held my hand and led me over to sit on the bench. He proceeded to tell me how he built the bench with his own hands for his daughter. She used to sit out there with him, and he would tell her jokes as they watched the stars and moon. I remember thinking to myself, this must be what he meant he wanted me to do for him. We would sit back on that bench for hours. He would tell me jokes, and we watched the stars and moon. After a while of silence, he placed his hand on my leg and rubbed back and forth up my thigh, and told me how beautiful I was, and that he had been watching me for a while. He said that he liked the way I carried myself, always like a lady; I wasn't fresh, hanging around boys. He said that there was a purity about me that made him feel close to me, then he picked up my hand, and kissed it. I remember getting that feeling again in the pit of my stomach. But I smiled, and said thank you. He smiled and said, "Let me get you home before your Momma starts looking for you." He took me by my hand, and led me back to the car. He told me to always make sure a man respects me the way that he does.

This continued over time, then one day he told me that he loved me, and he kissed me on the lips. I felt really special. He would buy me things: clothes, perfume, pocketbooks; basically, anything he wanted me to have.

He made me feel so special that one day when he told me that he loved me, I told him that I loved him, too. A tear gently rolled down his face as he leaned over to kiss me. But this time it was different, yet, oddly familiar. I felt like a bowl being licked after eating your favorite dessert. He embraced like the teddy-bear you gently pull close to you to go to sleep at night, and he unwrapped me like a beautiful gift to preserve the paper. I remember I kept looking at the stars in the sky as the tears rolled down my face; I felt gross. He was ever so careful with me. He picked me up, carried me to the car, and then drove to his house. He carried me inside the house, and placed me in the bath tub. He washed me, and helped me back into my clothes. Then he placed one finger over my mouth, and said, "This is our special love, and nooooo one must ever know about it."

Although he died later that night, I can still hear him in my hear till this day. His deep raspy voice still vibrates inside me. Hmmmm... I feel repulsed and my stomach is churning. I know what he did that night was not right, and that was not love...

Dear Diary,

Well, I am all checked in to my Junior Suite. Something about water always relaxes me, and I'm glad I have a great view of the river. I could not bring myself to stay with my family. I don't like being away from home; it's my safety net. Mainly, I miss my babies: Lexon, Zion, London, and Leroyce, Jr., who are my world. But, I have to be here. I am doing this for them, so I can be a better person for my husband, and myself.

I'll visit some of my family after I take a nap and freshen up. I need to get mentally prepared to deal with them, they are full of drama.

Uncle Elron is sitting on the front porch as Chastity pulls up to the house. She gets out of the car and his eyes were as wide as the front door was open, and his skin was pale as if he'd seen a ghost. He adjusted his glasses, and then he broke out with a big grin and said, "Chass, Chass, baby girl you sho' look just like yo' momma." They laugh and Chastity says, "Thank you, how are you Uncle Elron?" As they greet each other with a hug and kiss.

He points toward the house and says, "Yo' Aunt Rita is in da' kitchen cooking, go in there." Chastity opens the door, and goes inside. Looking around and thinking to herself how Grandma hadn't changed a thing; everything was exactly the same, even the curtains. The same brown curtains, the 70's velour wood living room set with the rocking chairs, and the table with the two cushions on the side. Chastity gigged inside "I never liked this furniture." Even the kitchen was the same: green appliances, old wood cabinets, with the curtain in front of the sink, and the countertops with the metal trim.

With a big smile she extends her arms to hug Aunt Rita and she says, "Uh uhh... I'm cooking Chass, you just came out dem streets. Wash yo' hands first." While Chastity washes her hands, Aunt Rita instructs her "and then split the ends off those beans."

"How you been baby?" she says, without lifting her head. Chastity gazes across the table at her and replies "I'm doing good, the kids are getting big, busy at work, that's all." She stares at her Aunt as she continues cooking, admiring the glimpses of her Momma and Grandmother in her face, hands, and mannerisms. Aunt Rita asks, "Why didn't you bring yo' family? Are you ashamed of us?" Chastity quickly replies, "No ma'am. I'm here to handle business remember; and I need to get some closure. My Momma said I could leave, and never come back, so that's what I did. But there are some things I feel I need closure on, so I am here to do that as well. Once I leave, I have no plans of coming back this way again. I'm sorry Aunt Rita, there's nothing here for me anymore." Aunt Rita angrily shouts, "We're here!" and she looks at Chastity with a stern face and continues to shout, "We're your family, and dem kids too." She got up and slammed the pot on the counter, turned towards Chastity and said with pain in her voice. "Damn it Chass, all you've ever done is run. I'm glad you're here and I pray you get the closure that you're seeking. But always remember this - like us, love us, or hate us, we're blood, and contrary to what you may think, we don't hate you, we love you." Chastity stands up, and walks toward the living room and says, "Well, y'all have always had a funny way of showing me and my Momma love. Y'all always blamed my Momma for everything wrong in your lives, and Grandma did too. I don't know what happened, I was too young, but whatever it was, y'all took it out on my Momma, and me too." Chastity walks out the front door, says bye to her uncle and leaves.

"Let me grab something to eat." Chastity says to herself as she drives past her old elementary school and high school. Chastity parks the car and goes inside the restaurant.

"Chass, Chass, is that you?" Chastity keeps walking, but the voice was getting closer. "Chass, girl I knew that was you, I know that walk anywhere. It's me Everett." Chastity removes her glasses and cleans them to refocus on his face, and finally it came back to her who he was, but not in a good way. Chastity says, "Everett, Everett Raymond?" He responds, "In living color, how you doing girl?" Chastity replies in disbelief, "My how you've changed. I'm well, what's going on with you?" He replies, "I'm doing really good. After I graduated from UCLA, I moved back out here to Detroit, I married Angela Mooreston, you remember her right, maybe not she's a few years behind us. Anyway, we got a couple kids, but we not together right now. You know, life happens, but I'm getting myself together now, and we're going to work it out. I got a job interview tomorrow over at MGM. What brings you to town? I clearly remember you telling me that you were never coming back this way?" Chastity tries to put on her most pleasant smile, and speak while holding her breath because he smells like a brewery mixed with sewage, and says, "Yes, that's true. My Grandmother passed, so I'm here for the funeral. It was nice seeing you. I hope things work out with you and Anna?" He quickly corrects her, "Angela." Chastity turns halfway back toward him and smiles and says, "Yes, my apologies, Angela. It really is nice seeing you again." He says, "Damn, you don't have to blow me off, I was just saying hi. You were always nice nasty, and you haven't changed, not one bit. Sorry to hear about your Grandmother. Take care, Chass," as he turns and walks out the restaurant.

Dear Diary,

I should have known this day was going left when I hugged my Uncle Elron and something felt uneasy in me.

I cannot believe I ran into Everett today. I'm so glad I broke up with him when we were leaving for college. That bum is someone else's headache and not mine. I'm not exactly sure what he said as he was walking away, but I think he said that I was still a controlling bitch.

What is with everyone saying that I am controlling? Is it a bad thing to have control? Money controls our lifestyle, diet controls our weight and illness, politics control education, war, and healthcare. There are things in life that need to be controlled. I don't understand why this is a reoccurring theme in my life.

I knew that this would be tough, but I know it's something that I need to do. It's amazing that after all these years, I still feel like an outcast. A part of me feels like I should not have come, but I know it's the right thing to do. Seeing them today has definitely brought up a lot of old emotions. Aunt Rita is right, I can't run forever. If I want a change, sometimes that means standing still.

Dear Diary,

I can't sleep. Seeing Everett reminded me of when I started high school; I was less than excited. Cass Tech was a HUGE building, and changing classes had me a little shook. The first week was a bit daunting, but I got through it. I got lost a few times, but I quickly got my route down, managed to get to class on time. Everett was in a few of my classes. He was tall, very handsome, and very athletic. I would follow him sometimes as we changed classes, and observed how the girls would be pursuing him. He would smile with those deep dimples, and reject them one by one. One day I seen his mother come to the school, and I saw how gentle he was with her, he even hugged and kissed her before she left, and he told her that he loved her. I remember thinking how sweet and caring he was. That's the type of man I want. Something about that exchange with his mother reminded me of Mr. Ron. He was polite, tender, and loving. I made it my quest to get to know him. Over the next few weeks I followed Everett's every movement. I checked out who he hung with, and the places he frequented. He only lived a few blocks from my grandmother's house, and his circle of friends were all clean-cut guys that stayed out of trouble. I remember it as if it was yesterday. I orchestrated the perfect moment for us to meet - at the skating rink.

Just as he was about to pass me, I conveniently turned and looked behind me, bumped into him, lost my balance, and fell on the floor. He was a gentleman, as I expected him to be. Everett was very attentive, tender, and sympathetic. He helped me up, held my hand, and led me over to a chair. He stayed with me and by the end of the night, we had exchanged numbers, and then we became high school sweethearts. He made me feel really special.

The years flew by, and the next thing I knew it was time for graduation, and we were heading off to college. I was going to Florida, and he was going to California. We both knew it wasn't going to work, and I broke up with him. I remember Everett sobbing, and saying, "Don't you want to at least give it a try?" I simply said, "Nope, I'm not coming back, and I don't want nothing holding me back from what the future has for me."

The decision wasn't hard for me. My Momma always told me to go away to college and that I didn't have to come back to Detroit. She wanted me to go and create a life for myself and be whoever I wanted to be. A week after graduation, on my eighteenth birthday, my Momma died. I felt completely lost and alone. The one person I trusted the most was now gone. Life was moving all around me, but inside me was the silence of my Momma's voice that death took from me. I would no longer feel her hugs, hear her advice, see her smile. She was the one person I always knew would be there for me. We did not always talk about everything, but she knew everything, and she always helped me to get passed my hurt, my anger, confusion, and my fears. My Momma had a way of making me smile and laugh even when she herself wanted to throw in towel and give up. In a lot of ways, we gave each other life.

I planned every detail of my Momma's funeral. I made sure every aspect truly reflected her personality. I even put her crack pipe and cigarettes in her cross-body purse and had it draped around her.

I remember watching as my Grandmother, and all of my mother's siblings sobbed at her funeral. I could hear my Momma saying, "They are going to miss me when I'm gone." This was the day; Elrena was now gone. That was the day I made peace with leaving too. I was determined that they were not going to use me, like they used my Momma. I left for college as soon as the dorm opened, and I never looked back.

I'm not looking forward to the reading of the Will tomorrow. But, I know this is all part of the process. I'm open to whatever it says, and I will do what needs to be done. My goal is to leave here FREE - from my pain, from my past, and free to move forward, never looking back.

Dear Diary,

I called home to check on Lee and my babies, and of course they are already complaining that Daddy is falling asleep, arriving late, and embarrassing them every chance he gets. As much as he prays, I wonder does he ever ask God to improve his home life? He makes it on time for court, on time for clients, but he's always late for family. I keep telling him family first, but we always fall further down on his agenda. I know one thing, he better be on time picking me up from the airport. He was rattling off a bunch of excuses, none of which I was interested in hearing. He's part of our struggle in this marriage too; it's not all me.

I'm going to listen to some meditations, and try to get some sleep. I have a full day tomorrow.

BREAKING CHAINS

The Lawyer says, "Chastity as your mother's only child you are entitled to your mother's portion of her inheritance from her mother's estate. The only asset she had was the house, which she left equally to all of her children." Aunt Rita and Uncle Elron both shout out with uttered excitement "where are we gonna live, we cared for her? She was supposed to leave the house to us, we cared for her?

Chastity interrupts and asks the attorney, "What do I need to do to get my name off the property." Uncle Elron shouts angrily, "Ain't nobody got no money to give you Chass. You just like yo' Momma always after the money." Chastity smiles, and says graciously, "I don't want any money, or any part of the house. I simply want out." The lawyer says, "If you're certain of your decision, I can draw up the paperwork, and have it ready for you to sign by tomorrow." Chastity nods in agreement and says, "I'm certain, they cared for her, they should have the house. I don't want any money from any of them. Let's think of this as my departing gift to you all." The lawyer waves for Chastity to follow him.

As her family watches her walk out they are stunned, clearly disturbed, and confused.

On their way to the secretary the lawyer asks again, "Are you certain you just want to sign over your share of the property? The property has value, and you are well within your right to request a buyout from the other owners for your share." Chastity says firmly, "I am absolutely positive. I don't want even a nail out of that house." He said, 'very well then."

Chastity arrives at the secretary's desk a bit distracted, the lawyer says something to the secretary and walks away, and smiles at Chastity and says, "She will take all your information and call you tomorrow when the papers are ready for you to sign. Chastity nods in agreement, and then his secretary leans forward on her desk and says, "Yes, he is fine, and sweeter than over ripe watermelon!" Chastity's eyes literally popped out her head, and she exclaims "What?!?" in disbelief she continues with sadness "That is so sad." The secretary nods her head in agreement and says, "Yeah, that's what his ex-wife said too when she caught him in bed with their neighbor. Another fine brother too, they live together now." Chastity drew her head back and mouthed, "Wow!"

Dear Diary,

The reading of the Will is done, and quite frankly, I'm surprised that my Grandmother had her affairs in order as well as she did. I believe I made the best

decision for me. I really don't want anything tying me back here to Detroit. If I hold
on to this property, it will just be a reason for them to call me. I want to leave with a
clear conscious. No strings, and no attachments.

I still cannot believe that that very dapper brother in his tailor fitted Armani brown
suit is gay. He was so fine with his silver hairline blending into his black hair. His
mustache was perfectly manicured, and his skin was the perfect shade of caramel; he
looked delicious. This is a perfect example of never knowing the true character behind
the veneer. It looks beautiful, shiny, and perfect. Yet it's a total contradiction.

Is this the story of my life? I look one way, but I'm completely deceptive?

Dear Diary,

Well everyday here has been triggers, and revelations. Today I got a chance to spend
some time with my Uncle Reece. He has always been full of bombshells, and today is
no different. He gave me a lock box that my Grandmother had hidden in her closet.
He said that it belonged to my Momma. He said, "I gave it to my mother when I
cleaned out you and your Momma's room after you went off to college. You left so
fast, you didn't even say bye to me." I said, "I'm sorry Uncle Reece, you were always
the coolest uncle, but whenever you were around Uncle Elron, Aunt Rita, and Uncle
Ray you would switch up. You went from protecting my Momma to turning on her. I
was always so bewildered by your tongue in cheek attitude; especially because I
remember how close you and my Momma was." He said, "I know, you know, but
they didn't know. Your Momma made me act like that to keep them off my back.
Because I was the quiet one, I could get by them with stuff, and they were none the

wiser. But my Mother knew, she always knew when I was up to no good." He laughed and said, "She always told me that one day I was going to get into trouble running drugs for Elrena. I would laugh, and tell her she didn't know what she was talking about. When I got into trouble, Elrena was dead and gone. Your Grandmother wouldn't even come to court with me. She was still blaming Elrena. She said she was the one that got me started. No matter what anybody said, Elrena was always to blame for everything that went wrong in this house. I am not sure why my Mother hated her so much. But I believe the answer is in that box. Your Momma held that box close to her, and no one has ever found the key. The local locksmith won't even open it. That's how much weight your Momma still got from the grave. Fred said he can only open it for you. That's what his Granddaddy told his Daddy, and his Daddy told him. It's even engraved on the bottom of the box, look at it." I turned the box over, and sure enough, that's exactly what it says. ONLY TO BE UNLOCKED FOR CHASTITY. *I gave my uncle a big hug, and he said, "Get on down there, and find out all things your Momma wanted you to know, but never had the heart to tell you. I'll be right here if you need me." I picked up the box, headed over to Fred's Key Shop, and they opened the box for me with no problem. But, I have yet to review what's inside. Something about the contents makes me feel very apprehensive. I'll open it later.*

Dear Diary,

I woke up this morning feeling very refreshed. I got a call from the attorney's office; the papers were ready for me to sign. I checked in at my office, and I got some work done. Before I knew it, the whole day had literally cruised by. Tomorrow is the funeral. I will say my final adieus to everyone, and it's time to head back to Florida.

I still don't have the peace I thought I would have, but I do feel that I am off to a good start.

Dear Diary

The funeral was beautiful. They laid Grandmother to rest with a service fit for a Queen. She had a beautiful white casket with gold trim, and praying hands insets outside the casket. The inside lining of the casket had embroidered praying hands. There was a beautiful afghan with a picture of her sitting in a chair with the quote, "Sit Down Servant" draped on the right side of the casket. She was dressed in a beautiful white dress, with lace accents, and she was adorned with gold jewelry. Her silver hair encased her face with curls. She looked so peaceful. The undertakers carried her casket on their shoulders, and rocked like a choir marching as they carried her out the church. They kept perfect timing to the music as the soloist sang, "I'm going up yonder to be with my Lord." The service was very upbeat, and celebratory. Those church folks loved my Grandmother. They spoke very highly of her. They seem to have a lot of respect for her. I wish I knew that woman.

At the Repast my Aunt Rita said that there is something she had to share with me before I leave. Her tone was very insistent, then she handed me an envelope and said, "This letter was written by my Mother. I made copies for all of us, and this one is for you. You have to read it, in your own timing." I put the letter in my purse, but I just pulled it out and read it.

My Dearest Children: Elron Jr., Elray, Elreece, and Elrita,

If you are reading this I have gone on to be with the Lord. I pray that every one of you are alive and well, and are present to hear, or read this letter.

I am writing this letter to set the record straight once and for all. To say the things, I could not bring myself to say when I was alive. The pain was too deep, and things had gotten so far gone that I could not get things back to where they should've been.

I was miserable with myself, and I was drinking, and drugging when y'all were kids. I felt a lot of despair. I had three children, no job, conceding my life to a man who abused me - to provide for me. My parents raised me better than that, yet I had allowed myself to plummet so low, that I no longer recognized who I was. I was just existing, no longer living. Your oldest sister Elrena was twelve at the time, she took care of you all much better than I did, and I resented her for that. She did everything that I told her to do, and she did it better than I could, and I absolutely despised her for that. I set out to destroy her for doing what I told her to do. After I had Elrita, I sunk into an even deeper depression. Elrena had just turned fourteen, and I began to turn her onto drugs too. I would have her go get them for me because I was too sick, weak, and embarrassed to go get them for myself. I would give her a little piece for going for me. My sickness caused her to drop out of school, and stay home with me to help take care of the four of you. We were broken, but she was all I had. Y'alls Daddy and I only were around each other long enough to fight and have sex. When Elrena became pregnant this caused a devastating break in our relationship, the reason for the rip she took to her grave, and I now take to mine.

Elrena gave birth to my first grandchild, Chastity Elrena, just before her 16th birthday. Now, there was seven of us in this three-bedroom house. We were both on welfare, drinking, and doing drugs. One thing I give Elrena credit for, she was functional. She took good care of all of you, and her own child. By the time all of you became of age, it was too late for Elrena to get clean. The only reason I got clean was because I had a stroke.

God saved my life, I went on to reinvent myself at church, yet I continued in my brokenness, and destroyed every one of you all's lives at home. I watched you all follow in our footsteps of drinking, drugging, hanging out in the streets, and I said nothing. It was easier to blame Elrena for y'alls addiction, and I silently blamed y'alls Daddy for mine. The truth is, I am the reason for it all. I did not know how to deal with my problems or my pain.

All those years, Elrena tried to tell y'all the truth, I would throw her out the house, and I would tell y'all she was lying - she was telling the truth. A truth so painful, a truth I could not bear to even whisper. When I gave my life to the Lord, I vowed that I would set the record straight. I gained part of my freedom when I wrote this letter. Although, I could not bring myself to share it while I was living.

I am so sorry for all the years of lying. I am so sorry that I allowed my own suffering, shame, and failure to leave you under a curse that was really meant for me. I am sorry that I pitted you all against each other. It was not the right thing to do. I figured if y'all were mad at each other, y'all would never talk to each other, and expose my truth.

Stop mistreating Chass. She is not to blame for what has happened in our family, and neither is Elrena, I am. She is simply looking for love, just as we all are. As my oldest grandchild I will always have a special love for her because of that. She was raised with you all, because her Momma was young when she had her, and your Momma is to blame for that too. Tell Chass I am so sorry.

I want to make things right, so the next chapter of your lives are no longer bound by the chains of my secrets and curses. Your father did not die in a car accident when I was pregnant with Elrita. Big Elron lives over by Chandler Park in McAuley Commons. Please go, and meet your father, he can tell you his truth; this is mine. Please go and meet him, and the rest of your family.

I should have never allowed my hurt, my depression, and my selfishness to destroy my family. I really do love you all, even if my poor judgment did not show it.

Love,
Mother

WOW!!! My Momma said it, she told me the truth, and nobody ever believed her; but I did. My aunt and uncles apologized to me. Now I understand why. I feel the chains   falling.   Thanks,   Grandmother

A PREDATOR IS BORN

Chastity arrives at the airport, and Lee is there with a huge smile and flowers waiting for her. Chastity says to him, "Why thank you, did you miss me?" Lee wraps his free arm around her lower back and pulls her in close and says, "You'll see just how much in a few minutes." Lee grabs her bags and takes her by the hand and leads her outside to a stretch limo. Inside he has her favorite wine on ice and the divider up. By the time they reached home, Chastity knew how much Lee missed her.

The kids ran to car, they are trying to open the doors, and yelling, "Mommy, Mommy." They finally get out the car and the kids were all over Chastity, and she is taking it all in. Lee brings her bags in and asks, "What's in this box?" Chastity says, "I'm not sure, I haven't looked in it yet, probably some old pictures and papers. It belonged to my Momma." The kids grab the box and begin pulling out the pictures asking Chastity, "Who is this Mommy?" Chastity is consumed with looking through the mail, says, "I'm not sure, y'all put everything back in the box, I need to go through it first." Reluctantly they put the pictures back and sadly say, "Okay." Chastity says, "It's time for a bath and let's get ready for bed." Lee comes up behind Chastity and asks, "Are you sure you're ready for bed?" Chastity swats the mail at him, smiles and says, "It's time to get some sleep, I'm tired." Lee retreats in defeat and slaps her on the butt.

Dear Diary,

I am so excited to be back home, to see my babies, my hubby, and to sleep in my own bed. My husband said that I appear to be more relaxed than normal, and maybe that trip was just what I needed. I feel some pressure off me, but I know there is more to deal with.

Today I want to talk about my college days. When I first moved on campus I was in the room by myself, as my roommate had not arrived yet. I encountered this tall, fine brother with a deep raspy voice, and a sexy laugh in the cafeteria. I could tell he was a ball player, not only was he a sky scraping 6 feet 7 inches tall, but he had that baller swag. I would sit in the corner, and watch him float through the various food stations to get his food, and as he sat with his teammates. I surveyed his interactions with them, how meticulous he was with placing the napkin over his lap, how intensely engaged he was in conversations, and how he maintained eye contact with whomever was talking. He was very neat. He would clean up his area, and properly dispose of all the garbage, and he would even reprimand his boys for leaving garbage behind. I liked his swag…he commanded respect, and others respected his authority. I purred like a cat on the inside…. I recall thinking to myself - He's gonna love me.

Over the next few weeks, I observed and followed him, being very careful not to be noticed. I was never too far behind, or to close. I learned his movements, his habits, his friends, and his hangouts. I arranged the perfect scenario for us to meet. It was a Free Wing Wednesday at the bowling alley, so he and his teammates always went bowling after practice on Wednesdays. I arrived early to walk through the plan. Like clockwork, they arrived at 9:00 PM. I was seated near the restrooms. When I saw him coming toward the bathrooms, I began walking in his pathway. When I got close, I looked down as if I had dropped my earring, conveniently bumping into him, and then I fell to the floor. He was extremely apologetic. He gently grabbed both of my hands and helped me up. I whined in pain. He gently held one of my hands, and placed his hand behind my back, and ushered me to the closest chair. He asked, "Are you ok, that was a pretty hard fall you took?" I replied, "I hope so. Didn't you see me?" I snapped and rolled my eyes. Then I said, "I probably need an X-ray." He swiftly offered to take me to the hospital stating, "We need to make sure you don't have a concussion." He then asked, "Are you by yourself?" I responded slowly, "No, I took the bus. And yes, I'm alone." He looked confused and said, "Cool, I'll be right back." I was holding my head while nodding ok. A few moments later he returned, he took me by the hand, and led me out the bowling alley.

I thought to myself - I'm in! He had a black on black Nissan Maxima with tinted windows. He was very careful with me, helping me into the car, and making sure I was buckled in. He got in and opened the sun roof, and it was a nice gentle breeze flowing through the car. It was clean, and it smelled like fresh vanilla. We headed towards the hospital, but as we got closer, I started looking in my purse, and asked, "Can you take me to my apartment, I need my insurance card." He said, "Sure." I directed him to the college, and he asked, "You live on campus?" I nodded yes. He said, "Me too. Why haven't I seen you around?" I shrugged my shoulders. He said, "Are you ok, you're not talking?" I said, "Yes, I just want to lay down." He said, "Oh boy, it's not good to lay down with a head injury. You have to stay awake for at least an hour. If you don't want to go to the hospital, I will stay with you, and make sure you stay awake for the next hour. This way we both know you don't have a concussion." He parked his car, came around to my side, opened the door, and extended his hand to help me out the car. I thought to myself, chivalry does still exist. He really made me feel worthy. When we got to my room I said to him, "My name is Chastity, what is your name?" he said, "Cheyenne, Cheyenne Miller, nice to meet you Chastity." I responded, "Likewise, Cheyenne Miller." We spent the next six hours talking about everything and nothing. He told me his truth, and I told him what I wanted him to know. He had been through a lot, and we actually had a lot in common. We both came from single parent households, raised by our mothers. His mother was still living; however, she is still struggling with addiction. He shared his hopes of making it to the NBA because he wants to save her from the streets. I saw this as a very admirable quality, and at the same time I felt sad for him because he doesn't know that he can't save her unless she wants to be saved.

Over the next few months we continued to talk, and on several occasions, I would conveniently be in the same place he was. I knew he had strong faith so I planted a seed and said, "Maybe this is a divine connection." He said, "You just might be right." We began to officially date midway into our freshman year.

Sophomore year in college was very difficult for Cheyenne. He tore his ACL and was out half of the basketball season. The day of his surgery, he received news that his mother passed from an overdose. I was right there for him, he was so broken. I decided to give him a ring to symbolize my love, and commitment to him. I wanted to assure him that no matter what, I would be there for him. That lifted his spirits, and firmly secured my influence over him. He was able to rebound from his injury, and he worked twice as hard in rehab to get back in the game for junior year.

Cheyenne was stoked. His dream was to be drafted into the NBA in the first round, and he made it. I was excited because I knew that we wouldn't have to struggle. My degree in Finance was about to be put to use big time, with long money.

Dear Diary,

Cheyenne and I were married at the court house right before he left for training in south Florida. We were able to find a nice condo, and I began a job as a Finance Project Manager. I was very conscientious with our spending so we could purchase a house. We were settling into life as best we could, considering our normal was not everyone else's normal. We had never seen what marriage really looked like, other than what we seen on TV. But our marriage still was very different because of his practice and travel schedule. I remember the first time Cheyenne was gone for a week, when he came home, I tied him to the bed and refused to untie him. He was yelling, so I put a tennis ball in his mouth. When I finally let him loose he said I was crazy, I told him, "Only for you." I told him that it was his fault, and that he made me that way. I apologized and promised never to do it again. He quickly forgave me, that's when I knew I had tamed him.

Cheyenne leans over Chastity and gives her a kiss and says, "I'm leaving for practice, but I'm going to be late tonight, we have a meeting after practice. Chastity says, "Ok love, I'll be waiting for you." Cheyenne goes to practice and after it was over he went to his boy Reek's house and says, "Man, something crazy happened last night. My wife tied me to the bed, put tennis ball in my mouth, and beat me like some dominatrix chick. That thing was crazy, I don't even know how to respond to that." Reek leans in with excitement and says, "Boy you crazy, a brother like me is looking for that type of freakism in the bedroom. You got a good wife, she did all that? I know you was up in that thing tearing it up." As he laughed and pushed Cheyenne on the arm. Cheyenne takes another shot and said, "You know I torn that thang up, but man, I wasn't expecting that, so at first it threw me off guard. She had the whole outfit on and everything. She had props. Man, if she like that and I'm gone a week, can you imagine what she's going to be like if I'm gone a month?" As he rubs his head in deep thought. Reek hands him another shot and says, "Yep, even freakier" and bursts out laughing. Then he says, "Seriously man, if I were you, I would embrace it. Live in the moment and treat it like we treat the strippers in the clubs, and the tricks in our rooms on the road. Apparently, she wants to give it to you at home so you won't cheat on her on the road. Its reverse that psychology. You're a lucky man, you can get freaked on the road and at home. Yep, I'm jealous." Cheyenne takes another shot and says, "You know what, you right. That's exactly what she's doing. I'm gonna ride this thing out, I got the best of both worlds, and I can't be mad at her for that. Matter fact, I'm going home to hit that thang right now. Yo' bro I'm out. Thanks for listening." Cheyenne daps up his boy and goes home.

Chastity is fast asleep when he gets home. He tries to wake her up, and she says, "Where was the meeting at? Joe's Tavern? you smell like Hennessy. Go shower, good night. I'll wake you in the morning or something." Cheyenne laughs and stumbles around the bed saying, "It's like that now, last night you were all over me, tonight you don't want to be near me? I'll take a shower, but then I'm going to tear that thang up, I'm hooked." Chastity smiled with her back to him and tooted her butt up a little higher in the bed and said, "I'll be right here when you get out the shower. Make sure you brush your teeth and gargle. I got something for you Mr. Hooked." Cheyenne did just as she said, but when he laid across the bed he fell fast asleep. Chastity laughed and rubbed from his face to his groin area and whispered, "Got him!"

The next time he was gone for a month, when he got home he volunteered to be tied up. Chastity obliged him and played nice for a while. She felt something was off, so she waited for him to get home so they could share the moment of her taking a pregnancy test. Cheyenne laid his bags in the closet and was preparing to get in the shower. Chastity was in her robe waiting for him in the bathroom with the pregnancy test on the counter. Cheyenne looked at the test, looked at her and ask, "Are you serious? I'm going to be a father? Chastity replied, "We're about to find out." She began opening the packaging and after she urinated on the stick, she gave it to him and says, "I'll let you tell me the results and we'll take it from there. She gave him a deep passionate kiss and went into the bedroom. A few minutes later Cheyenne appeared from the bathroom beat red with tears running down his face. He was holding the test up in front of him so Chastity could read it as he tried to say, "I'm going to be a.... Da...Da...Daddy.... we 're - we're going .... to be.... parents." He grabbed Chastity and began to kiss her all over her body. Chastity became furious and she spanked him. Cheyenne responded with delight as usual this was their game. But the more trips he went on the more enraged Chastity was when he got home and their game became more violent, and wild. Chastity's hormones were in overdrive and so was she.

Cheyenne is hanging out with his boy Reek and he tells him, "Man, since she got pregnant she's even more wild. I'll be glad when the baby gets here. I feel like my knees are going to buckle." Reek laughs and tells him, "Hang in there boy, pregnant sex is the best sex. Well, at least that's what I've been told anyway. I ain't got no kids and I ain't trying to have none."

When Lexon was born, and he became the new love of Chastity's life. She no longer wants Cheyenne to touch her; instead she wants to continually punish him. Cheyenne *ass-sumed* she was going to stop with this craziness after her hormones were back under control. But Chastity enjoys watching him quiver as she beats him. She became even more aroused at the sight of him crying, and his pleas for her to stop. Chastity relishes at putting the tennis ball in his mouth, silencing him, and all he could do is use his eyes to communicate with her. She asks, "Do you want to call for help? Do you wish you could call your Mommy? Lexon's Mommy is here for you." As she sits on his chest, and breast feeds Lexon.

Dear Diary,

I am not sure why watching him in pain brought me so much joy? But no matter what I did he always came back home; he was very obedient. Although my actions had minimal impact on my erotic stimuli, it did soothe my psyche. I felt much better after I beat him, I found pleasure in having him mute, and helpless. So did he apparently, he literally would explode within seconds of insertion.

I remember one night we went out to dinner with Reek and one of his many chicks. I couldn't believe the slick comment made - he said, "I better be quiet, I don't want a whooping." He tried to make a joke of it and elbow up his boy and laugh, but I caught it and he did too. I quickly replied, "That's right, you know how much I enjoy giving them." It was really awkward, probably because I licked my lips, bit my lower lip, and purred like Eartha Kitt. But that night he crossed a line with me. I felt a breach in out trust, and I felt compelled to show him I did not appreciate the bed of affliction being exposed. When we got home, I took him in the chamber., and let's just leave it here…. he could barely walk the next day. I bet he was grateful the season was over.

Dear Diary,

When the new season began, life began to unravel. Everything fell apart - Cheyenne's NBA career took a downward turn. Cheyenne began drinking more, hanging out more, and eventually slipped up and cheated on me - IN MY FACE AND IN MY BED! That's a bold demon if I ever saw one. He thought it would be cool to invite a guest into the chamber. When I arrived home Cheyenne and some chick was in the thick of things. Cheyenne says to me, "Madam, why don't you join us." I remember my lips quivered with fury and I hissed at him like a wild cat preparing for attack, then I said, "Sure, don't mind if I do." His new friend seemed to become more titillated by my response. She got off of Cheyenne, and sat up on her knees inviting me in as if she was at home. I said to her, "I'll be right back sweetie." I put Lexon down for his nap, and put on my gear. Cheyenne was laughing, and exciting himself with her as he continued to drink excessively. I came into the room wearing my corset, boots, and mask. I pulled the bed into the middle of the floor, and proceeded to tie them together, laying on their sides with their backs to each other. I turned the music up so the neighbors wouldn't hear their screams. Slowly I appealed to their senses rubbing a feather across their bodies to stimulate them as if I was really interested in indulging intimately with them. Then I flipped and I began to lash them with the riding crop. The sting from the strikes made them convulse like fresh fish out of water. I then rolled them on their stomachs and began ravaging their skin with fire. The more they flinched from the flames, the angrier I became, and I whipped them with the flogger. The more I swung, the more my anger escalated. I turned Cheyenne onto his back and sat on his chest and asked him, "Are you thirsty baby?" as I poured the liquor down his throat. He was gagging and coughing as it overflowed from his mouth. I threw what was left on the girl and asked sarcastically, "You want some too?" The girl closed her eyes and turned her head. I sat back on the bed near the foot between them laughing at them as I dug my stiletto heels into their bodies. I picked up the lighter again and said, "It can all be over in a flick of a Bic." Cheyenne was so intoxicated he couldn't make a decent sentence. The girl was basically eye pleading for her life. I said to her, "It's not about you. I'm not into women. It's about his disrespectful ass." I untied the girl, and told her, "I'm not going to allow his temporary poor decision to be a permanent change to my life or yours. He's not worth it."

I knew after that day that our marriage was over. I transferred most of the money from our account into my private account. I packed up me and Lexon, and moved back to Orlando. Within eighteen months it had all fallen apart.

I know I played a big part in the demise of my marriage, it wasn't all him. Once I opened the chamber, a new part of me was born and it was hard to tame that side of me. We all have demons, but once we relinquish control to them, it's hard to regain control back.

That day something broke inside of me, and I couldn't go back. I was always adventurous and willing to try new things, but, women have never been my interest, *and I have never been interested in sharing my husband with another woman! I always wondered what he was thinking? But, I never cared enough to find out.*

That's enough for tonight; this is intense.

Dear Diary,

I have to say since my trip to Detroit things have improved between Lee and I. I know I still have work to do. But I now realize that he and Mikayla were right, I needed the counseling first alone. In a few weeks he will start his personal sessions then we will merge together.

My baby, Leroyce, Jr., isn't feeling well, I need to take care of him. No matter how well we are doing, if I leave it up to Lee, I will be up all night with two babies —
Senior   and   Junior.

THE KING

Dear Diary,

Ok, I have a few minutes before I need to take London to dance class.

Over the next few years, I focused on rebuilding a solid foundation for me and Lexon. I decided to go back to college, and get my Master's Degree. I did not want to date during that time. I couldn't take a chance on my past showing up. I needed to be focused so I could finish. That's when I met Mikayla and hired Consuela. The purpose of me getting a roommate was so I could afford to hire a nanny for Lexon. Consuela is like a member of my family. She has been with me since Lexon was almost two.

Consuela is from the Dominican Republic, and had been in this country for about twenty-five years. She specializes in house management and child care. She has two children of her own, who are both married and have children of their own back in the Dominican Republic. Both of her sons moved back, and started businesses there to help other family members have a better life. Consuela says she prefers America, because she makes better money here, and she doesn't have to work as hard. She has become one of my dearest friends as well.

Time to go! Will write more later.

Dear Diary,

After college graduation, I began working for one of the top financial companies in the world. My first week on the job I was assigned a new client, and a new team. We were all new, so that made it an easy adjustment. No "old" attitudes for the new boss to contend with. I specifically chose Craig to travel with me to meet the new client. There was something about him that intrigued me. While there I took him out for dinner so I could get to know him better. He was single, a few years younger than me. He was from the local area, and had tons of family nearby. That's was a turn off to me. I like men that are more like me - loaners. When they have a lot of family connections, it really complicates things. They always want to come over, hang out, know your business, and all that kind of stuff. I didn't want to share my time, or my man's time, with other people. I just wanted it to be me and him, and our children if we have any. So, once I found out that he had a lot of family near him, I quickly shifted, and kept things very professional. He is still one of my top employees. I have now been employed with the company for over ten years. I love my job!

Dear Diary,

Sorry about last night, Lee came in, and I got side tracked. There is never a dull moment with Lee, and I never know what to expect day to day. I guess this is another reason that I am attracted to him, he's a mystery to me at times. Last night he came home super excited. He had flowers, and gifts for everyone in the house, including Consuela. He was dancing and singing, my initial thought was: what has he been drinking? Then he said, "Everyone get dressed we are going out to dinner." Please note, I don't like going out to dinner with him, his etiquette is not the best. But, he insisted that we all get dressed up, so we did. He took us to a very nice upscale restaurant. Not only was dinner great, but his manners at the table were impeccable. This is not so easy to say, I can find fault in a corner. Well, he announced that not only did he win a big case in court, but that his commission was exactly what he needed to open his own firm! Well, that's when everything went to hell in a hand basket for me. I had a ton of questions, and I went in full throttle, "Where will your office be? Who are your clients going to be? How long is it going to be before you start making money? Certainly, you don't think you're going to live off of my money? Run your firm off of my money? You're always coming up with these grand ideas, and never thinking about the important details." Needless to say, the party ended there. Lee said, "I think it's time to go. Mom and I have some grown folks' things to discuss in private." The ride home was completely silent. Lee stayed in the car once we arrived home. Everyone went inside and went directly to their rooms, including me. Once Lee came inside, he came straight to me, took me by the hand, and said, "Listen, I didn't marry for your money, or Ezekiel's money. I married you because I love you. You're always talking about I need to pray for time, well I did, and God has answered my prayer and is giving me more time as the owner, not forced to work the hours someone else has assigned to me. You need to trust me, trust the God in me, and let me be the man God is calling me to be. I have never asked you for a dime, and never will. I am my own man, I make my own money, and I always pay my own way. I pay all the bills in this house, and I give you whatever you want and more." The most touching part for me and I am not very religious. He said, "I am the head of this family, like Christ is the head of the church. Sometimes you have to submit to His will, trust His leading, and watch Him do what only He can do. He has appointed me to do this, and I can do this." Well, I was speechless, I felt faint and rescued at the same time. He's never spoken to me with such confidence and firmness before. Then he told me that he has been taking etiquette classes during his lunch break so I won't be embarrassed when we go out to eat, or host parties for his new clients. He has definitely stepped into his own man, I like it, and I think I will keep him. I had to give him some extra love, he deserved it!

Lee took a moment in the car and called out to God, "What is wrong with this woman? Why does she always have to be so difficult? Why is she always accusing me of wanting her money? Lord doesn't she know that what you have given, you can surely take away? Lord why does she always attack my manhood? I feel like she's trying to make feel less than a man. Lord you said that I am more than a conqueror, you said I am the lender not the borrower. Lord you said now's the time to pursuit. Lord I need your spirit to give me the boldness to cover this family as Christ covers the head of the church. I need you to fill me up to overflow. Lord, I need you because I cannot do it by myself.... I thank you, I hear you. I am not anxious, because I know you are with me. I do not have a spirit of fear, but of power, love, and self-control. I am your chosen son, a royal priest, peculiar... I shall run and not get weary, walk and never faint, I will mount up on wings like and eagle and fly above the storm. I will win, because you called me friend. Thank you,

Lord, I hear you Lord, and I'm going to tell her Lord, right now. Thank you, hallelujah, God you are greatly to be praised, you are my strength and my shield. Glory to your name Father. Amen."

Dear Diary

Today I feel the need to share about Ezekiel, my late husband. From the moment I met him there was something different about him. I would call him "My King". He and I connected on a kingdom level. He was the only man to ever rule over me. I'll never forget the day I met Ezekiel. He pulled up next to me on his motorcycle. All he was wearing was a helmet, shorts, and unlaced boots. He was glistening with sweat, and his body was cut in all the right places. When the light changed, he took off, and I was hot on his trail. I don't know why, but I was. I felt a strong urge to know him, and all his vital statistics. So, I followed, and a few turns later he pulled into the garage of a beautiful bungalow. I remember feeling overwhelmed with shyness, and I kept going.

Over the next few days I would ride by on my way home, nothing, no sign of him anywhere. I started thinking, "maybe that's not where he lives, maybe he was visiting a friend." I finally saw him again in the store at the gas station. I paid for my items ahead of him, and I waited for him to come out the store. This time he was in a car. I followed him again, and he went to the same house. I came back later that night, and I watched all night. The next morning, he appeared from the garage alone. I followed him to the hospital. I stayed there all day to see if he was picking anyone up, or actually working there. After about four hours, he came out in scrubs, got something out of his car, and went back inside. I patiently waited, another six hours passed. He came out, got in his car, and headed out. I followed him to the gym, to the grocery store, then back home. No lights were on inside the house until he arrived, so he must live alone. I went home and slept well that night; I was exhausted.

I continued over the following weeks to periodically ride through the hospital parking lot looking for his car, or motorcycle. I would check the gym, the grocery store, and his house. His routine was pretty basic. I coordinated the perfect moment for us to meet at the grocery store. I pretended to be looking at the vegetables, and not paying attention to him behind me, and back up right into his cart. "Ouch" I proclaimed as I grabbed my ankle. He quickly came around his cart saying, "I apologize, I didn't see you standing there. Are you ok? Let me look at it, I'm a doctor." I continued to rub my ankle and said, "Really, a doctor, that's a good line. You broke my ankle, and that's the best line you could come up with?" He said, "No, really I am. I work in the ER at the hospital across the street. I have no reason to lie. My name is Dr. Mohammed, Ezekiel Mohammed. Let me look at it and make sure you're okay." He looked at me with those puppy eyes, and gently took my hand off my ankle, and said, "You're a little red, but you should be fine. The skin isn't broken. Just a flesh wound." He stood up, extended his hand to me, and said to me, "How can I make it up to you?" "Well, Dr. Mohammed, dinner would be nice. Do you cook?" He laughed and said, "Yes, I'm actually a great cook." "Great, I'm an excellent food critic." We both laughed. I was totally enthralled with his rich deep chocolate skin, succulent lips, and perfectly sculptured arms twinkling like stars in the sky on a clear summer night. His smile lit up the room like candles at an intimate dinner, and my heart fluttered like a butterfly breaking free from a cocoon. I knew from the beginning, he was the one. We made plans to meet for dinner that Thursday night at his place. He said that he lives alone, and most of his family lives up north. He came down here because he was tired of the cold weather. He wanted to be able to ride his motorcycle all year around. That brief introduction was the confirmation that I needed, YES, he is the one.

I'll write more tomorrow, Zion needs help with an assignment.

Dear Diary,

After a year of dating we were married, we moved into his house, and life began to move for me in a different way. Ezekiel stimulated me intellectually in ways that I have never been. Our conversations were riveting, intense, and encompassed a broad range of topics. Every day was new with him. He had style, grace, and presence. No matter where we went he commanded attention, and we were always the main attraction. He was well respected by his colleagues, and all their wives fawned over me. It was like, the party didn't start until we arrived. No matter where we were in the world his very presence changed the atmosphere. He was a King, and I was his Queen. He took care of his family, not financially, but emotionally. They never made decisions without consulting him first. He was not only a gifted doctor, he was brilliant with finances. He knew exactly when to buy, and when to sell. He knew how to work with his hands. He lived life worry free. He was a natural leader. We never argued, he would say his peace, and there was peace. I got it, I felt it, and I understood it. Oft times I would find myself apologizing to him, and he would just smile, kiss me, and say, "It is well love."

Oh, how I long to hear those words. I miss him so much.
I have to go… this is as far as I want to go right now.

Dear Diary,

Ezekiel was a very special man. He didn't have just physical strength, but an inner strength that overpowered, and ruled me. I was willing to submit to him. I tried to introduce him to the chamber, and he wanted no parts of it. I got in my gear, and came out the bathroom with my feather behind my back. I climbed on top of him and began to gently rub it on his thigh. He quickly flipped me onto my back, leaned down as if to kiss me, and whispered in my ear, "I don't play like that." He got up off me, and went into the shower. I wasn't quite sure how to respond. I was accustomed to having things my way. In this moment I felt rejected and humiliated. I followed him into the shower, apologizing, and trying to save face like I was only playing. He refused to play at all. I yielded to the traditional roles of marriage, and participated in the missionary, and doggy style positions. As long as he was pleased, I was satisfied in the moment because making him happy mattered. But, soon I found myself on the hunt for a muse. I could not escape the overwhelming desire to be in the chamber, to whip, dominate, and destroy. There was something about the position of rulership that excited me, soothed me, and calmed me. I wasn't content being submissive. It wasn't resolving my inner beast that was desperately fighting to come out, if only for a moment. I needed to release that painful pleasure that was rising inside me. Although he was my King, he ruled over me, he was unable to tame the inner most part of me. After a while, I found myself on the prowl... and there was no turning back.

"Lord I thank you!" Lee proclaimed after his meeting with the counselor. He continued saying, "Lord I knew I wasn't crazy, not that I'm saying my wife is, but Lord I needed an answer and you have never failed me. The wait was worth it. Daniel hit the nail on the head when he said, "The reason your wife degrades you is because she feels degraded internally; she is in internal conflict and turmoil. So, lashing out at others is her subconscious way of making herself feel better, so she thinks. Once the moment goes away, so does the victory." Lord I feel better, thank you for enlarging my territory today, I felt maxed out, yet again, you stretched my capacity of understanding from her point of view so I can properly respond to her. Thank you Lord, Ha sha la ba ba ba. You are a gracious God, always on time God. I know it's going to get better God, Thank you."

Lee goes in the house with power and authority. "Good Afternoon Love." he says to Chastity. She replies on cue, "Good Afternoon King." Lee said, "That I am, Queen. Business is picking up, God is faithful. I am on track to break six figures in six months." Chastity stands up and walks over to Lee and says, "That's awesome King, I knew you could do it. You're exceeding my projections, and I must serve you well before the kids get home." Lee did not waiver in his stature, he said, "Shut the door." As she proceeded on his command she asked, "How was the counseling?" He replied, "It's private, you'll have to wait until our joint sessions to know what's going on." He pushed her to her knees she did not disappoint. The continued in the shower, and they were mutually served.

THE PROPHECY FROM THE MUSE

Dear Diary,

One day the doorbell rang and there he was, asking for my signature for a certified letter. The perfect muse, was there before my eyes. He was very militant, straight to the point, and task centered. I liked that about him. I began imagining in my mind how I could subdue him, and have him submit to my wants, desires, and commands.

A few days had passed, and I still could not get him out of my mind. I knew then, I had to have him. So, I began constructing the perfect plan for us to meet again. I arranged for Consuela to be out of the house on some errands. I had several boxes sent to my home that would require him to bring them inside for me. This was the perfect opportunity to get him inside, and spend a few minutes with him. While all the cats are way, I will play!

My plan worked beautifully! He arrived on-time, and told me he had quite a few packages for me. I asked him if he could bring them into my office, and as expected -

he politely obliged. I conveniently tripped over one of the boxes, and he quickly reached out and caught me before I fell. He said, "Please be careful, we can't have you falling on my watch. Are you ok?" I said, "Yes, But I may have twisted my ankle a bit, I'll be ok." He said, "You should get some ice on it right away." He took my hand and laced my arm around his neck, and helped me over to my chair. I pointed to the First Aid kit, he opened it, activated the ice bag, and gently placed it on my ankle. He said, "This is going to be cold but, it will definitely make you feel better." I said, "Thank you, Sir." He said, "No problem ma'am. My name is Dwayne by the way. Just remain seated, and I will get the rest of your packages." After he finished bringing in all the packages, I said to him, "How can I ever repay you for all your kindness? lunch or dinner?" He smiled and said, "No payment required, I'm just doing my job ma'am." I said, "Saving a lady from falling is a part of your job? They must pay you very well at the Post Office." We laughed, and he replied, "Well, that quick response comes from my military training." I quickly interrupted him because I knew Consuela would be arriving soon. I handed him my card and said, "Call me tomorrow, and we will set it up. No excuses, I insist." Obedient, just as I knew he would be, he called me, and we made plans to meet for lunch.

Then, I implemented phase two on my plan. I watched his moves, where he went, and who he hung out with. He was pretty much a loner. He worked, went to the gym, and then home. He lived by himself, no girlfriend, or roommate.

Now, I was sure that he was the perfect muse for my midday chamber snack. I called him and asked if I could bring him lunch, this time I requested to meet at his place, since he had already been to mine. I arrived on time, and we began meeting during his lunch break. There were days he would take half days because he said he needed more time in the chamber.

I'll continue this later, I have to take the kids to a party today. It's amazing, Lee said starting his own firm would give him more flexibility, yet I never see that extra time when it comes to the kid's activities. I have to make a note on that for our joint counseling sessions. I'm still getting the longer end of the stick on this one.

Dear Diary,

Let's continue. I preferred going to Dwayne's place because he had a private entrance. I purchased new gear and kept it there. He had an average bachelor pad with the basics. Black leather reclining sectional with a trunk coffee table. A huge TV inside the black glass entertainment center, which was filled with an extensive CD and DVD library. He had a basic five-piece black glass kitchen table and chairs. Everything was always clean and in order. His bedroom had black blackout curtains, another huge TV on the TV stand, along with another CD and DVD player for continued entertainment in the bedroom. He had an iron four poster bed that sat in the middle of the floor, and was laced with sheer black panels. He had candles all around the room sitting at various heights. He also liked to wear gear, especially the mask. The first few months I entered his chamber and methodically took charge. I quietly stripped him of his power and isolated him from outside interactions. I became his workout, he no longer needed the gym. He was strong, yet intellectually complex. He was the perfect muse, and equally stimulating mentally. He was not afraid of me, yet he was lost in me. After we had been seeing each other for about a year, I gave him a wedding band. I told him that it symbolized our chamber marriage. I demanded that he wear it every day, and I gave him strict orders on what he could and could not do with other women. He was very loyal, and very obedient.

One of our most exciting experiences was the day he called me and said that he wanted to meet me at my house. I said sure, my husband was out of town at a convention, and Lexon was in school all day. I gave Consuela some errands that would take her out the house all day. He said this time he felt led to do something different. I changed into my riding gear and he assumed his position. But this time, he had the Bible with him, he opened it and laid it on the floor and he began to read....

"How beautiful your sandaled feet, O prince's daughter!
Your graceful legs are like jewels, the work of an artist's hands.
Your navel is a rounded goblet, that never lacks blended wine.
Your waist is a mound of wheat encircled by lilies.
Your breasts are like two fawns, like twin fawns of a gazelle.
Your neck is like an ivory tower.
Your eyes are the pools of Heshbon by the gate of Bath Rabbim.
Your nose is like the tower of Lebanon looking toward Damascus.
Your head crowns you like Mount Carmel. Your hair is like royal tapestry;
the king is held captive by its tresses."

I don't know why, but his words infuriated me; the more he read, the more violent I became, and I unleashed full throttle on him. His skin welled up forming blisters, yet he continued to read...

"How beautiful you are and how pleasing, my love, with your delights!

Your stature is like that of the palm, and your breasts like clusters of fruit.

"I will climb the palm tree; I will take hold of its fruit."

May your breasts be like clusters of grapes on the vine, the fragrance of your breath like apples, and your mouth like the best wine."

The more he read, the harder I swung. He didn't move, not even a flinch. It was as if he was determined to get every word out.

There was a knock at the door. It was Consuela asking if everything was ok. I yelled to her that everything was good. I listened for her bedroom door to close. He changed positions, and he started to recite from memory.

"The Lord is my shepherd, I lack nothing. He makes me lie down in green pastures, he leads me beside quiet waters, he refreshes my soul.

He guides me along the right paths, for his name's sake.

Even though I walk, through the darkest valley,

I will fear no evil, for you are with me;

your rod and your staff, they comfort me."

I could tell he was tired, but even in his weakness, he arose for me. Strong like a piston in an engine; I went along for the ride. Yet, nothing ignited, no combustion… I was completely void of spark. I continued to strike, his skin-popped liked grapes, and his lips shivered as if he was out in the cold. He bit his bottom lip, and took a deep breath in, and a long exhale out as if he was recapturing some strength to take more.

He continued to impart the words to me, and I moved as if my skin was in fire. His words felt like they were piercing me, as if I was being punished.

"You prepare a table before me in the presence of my enemies.
You anoint my head with oil; my cup overflows.
Surely your goodness and love will follow me all the days of my life,
and I will dwell in the house of the Lord forever."

I was determined to bring him to where I wanted him to be, and he exploded. It was the first time I'd ever heard the word of God expressed so poetically; yet, it rested deeply in me and it frustrated me at the same time. I told him to never do that again, it wasn't the place for that.

After that night, things changed for us. I no longer wanted him in my chamber, and I had no desire to be in his.

Something disconnected us that day. I felt like every time we saw each other; he was always preaching to me. He kept saying that God had so much more for me. Our encounters severed that part of me from him, and had me avoiding his calls. Finally, one day I told him that the game was over, and it was time for him to move on. It was as if my words fell on deaf ears. He was obsessed with me. I told him, he would never own me, I am a married woman. He kept saying that God was speaking to him, and that he had been assigned to tell me things. The problem was, I wasn't a believer, and I certainly wasn't interested in what God had to say unless he was telling Dwayne to leave me alone. Especially at that moment – that's all I wanted Dwayne to do, and for his God to help him to do it. After a few weeks of dead-end requests and conversations, I called the Postmaster and had his route changed to Mikayla's neighborhood. I figured in her desperation for a man, that she would meet him and take him off my hands. After all she is beautiful, single, and successful. A lot of men were very attracted to her, all she had to do was not tell him she was a virgin on the first date and she'd be straight; but, because he continued to wear that damn ring, she slammed the door in his face every day. I was so irritated every time she would tell me about it. I would encourage her to just talk to him, maybe he wears it for a different reason. I even called Dwayne and asked him for the ring back; he refused. He said not until I heard him out.

Well, in the midst of all this I found out that I was pregnant. Ezekiel was elated to say the least. He called his family up north, and they began making plans to visit around the time the baby is due. We started renovating one of the bedrooms to turn it into the nursery.

But Dwayne, he was relentless in his pursuit to tell me what "God" supposedly had assigned him to tell me. He called, he sent emails, he begged, he pleaded with me to meet him in person. He said that he could not give me this "word" over the phone, only in person. So, I reluctantly agreed to meet with him. But I told him that it had to be in a public place. I didn't want to take any chance that things could possibly go further with us. My life was moving forward with Ezekiel, and I was determined to be faithful to him. I also wanted my family firmly committed by the time this baby was born, come hell or high water.

So, I met with Dwayne at the food court in the mall. We sat down and he proceed to tell me, "The Lord said that the wrath of judgement is over your house. The things that you aspire to do, only He can do. This encounter was a divine intervention. In three days, your house will fall, and you will live in ashes and ruin until you submit to Him. You claim to be the ruler, but He is the true ruler. Just as He has given, He will take away. Heed the word of the Lord, turn from wickedness, and He will deliver you with a new mind, a new heart, and a new name." When he finished, he was in tears. I began to clap my hands and say, "You should be an actor, you almost had me convinced. All that reading the bible, coming to me with this so-called "message" from the Lord, I don't believe one word of it. What wrath is over my house? What does that mean? A storm is coming, and going to blow my house down? I'm going to live in ashes and ruin. Is there going to be a fire or something? Yeah ok, I came, I listened, now can I have the ring back please?" He wiped away his tears, stared me straight in my eyes and said, "Is the baby mine?" My mouth dropped to the floor. I thought to myself, how in the hell does he know, I never told him I was pregnant. I pushed my chair back from the table, and replied with anger and restraint, "Hell No!" and walked away. When I got in my car, I felt like I was going to hyperventilate. The truth of the matter was, I didn't know whose baby it was. But, because I was married, it was my husband's baby. I felt overwhelmed, and I feel that way right now all over again. Two days after that meeting, Dwayne accidentally killed my husband because I chased him out of my house.

I need a break. I will write more later.

UNVEILING THE MASK

Dear Diary,

It's amazing to me as I re-read my previous entries not only did Dwayne know I was pregnant with Zion, but he also knew I wanted to change my name. I was so furious with him, I could not hear him. Within three days my whole life was ashes and ruin. I was planning my King's funeral, pregnant, and he was going to prison. Truthfully speaking, I still don't know who Zion's father is. I can see traces of Ezekiel and Dwayne. At this point, It is a mute-point that does not need ever be addressed. Zion's father is deceased, and it's best kept that way. Moving on....

Dear Diary,

I finally looked through the lock box. When I first opened it, I became very emotional looking at all the pictures of me when I was a baby, toddler, elementary school, junior high, and high school. My Momma had a picture of her for every year that she had one of me. We look like twins (laugh). There were letters to my Momma from a man named Mike, who was in the military. The letters expressed his deep love for her. He wanted to marry her, but was broken hearted when she turned him down.

The biggest and most devastating find… was my Birth Certificate. It listed my Daddy's name: Elron Beard, Sr. I read it over, and over, and over again. This can't be right. This can't be true. My Daddy, is my Granddaddy?!? This was the rip that my Grandmother was talking about in her and my Momma's relationship. There it was in the box, all the way at the bottom: Pictures of my Momma, and her Daddy, sitting on the bench, by the pond…the same bench, the same pond, the same Mr. Ron. HE PREYED ON MY MOMMA! HE PREYED ON ME! HE DID IT TO MY MOMMA! HE DID IT TO ME!

My demons are monstrous, and they run deeper than oceans are wide. I have come to the realization that I am my father's child. I am a predator too. The patterns in my life are very similar to the behaviors I experience with him. He preyed on me, and I preyed on others. We are cut from the same cloth. I believe that my mother knew what happened to me and that's why she told me that he died. This is still blowing my mind, and making me sick at the same time.

MY WHOLE LIFE I HAVE BEEN LIVING A MASQUERADE!!!
I've been presenting myself as this one character, but the true essence of my profile is a "predator." I take calculated steps to get near my victims by following them, watching them, learning their habits, and moves. I choose victims that are isolated and alone, so I can keep them to myself, so I can possess them, own them, control them. I carefully orchestrate meetings, gain their trust, and then I attack them. He taught me that behavior - he did it to me, I did it to them, and it's in my DNA. Yuck! I

have often spoken about Chass as if she was someone else, but in actuality; I am she, she is me, and we are one. I didn't want anyone to call me Chass because I thought it was an eerie reminder of where I was from. But I am still here, Chass and Chastity. I'm a mess, a broken mess. Now I see the fractured soul that my husband and Mikayla have peered into and are constantly praying for. I have reached rock bottom, the ashes and ruin that Dwayne told me about are here at my door to the very essence of everything I thought I was.

Lee keeps saying to me that the problems he has with our marriage are my sense of entitlement, and my need for power and control. He said that I am unable to connect with him intimately and emotionally. That I always blame others when things go wrong instead of owning responsibility for what I did. Lee said that I have no compassion for people, that I am mean, and my words are harsh. I never thought these things were true about me. My defense was - people like me, they say I'm nice, and people are drawn to me, I just don't let them in.

As the tears hit my iPad, and I dry them with my shirt, I realize that I have been violated in the deepest part of my soul. That I not only have been operating, and shielding a lot of hurt, pain, and abuse from my childhood, but that I am also an abuser. I am a living fraud. I get up in the morning and put on my face, wear my designer suits, and go on with life as if the past has never happened to me. As if I've never done anything to anyone else. It's all a lie. I'm a PREDATOR - I'm living a daily MASQUERADE!!!

It really doesn't matter what anyone else knows about me, or says about me. It's what I think about me, how I feel about me. I never took time to assess how I felt about me. I knew I was ugly, but I am downright disgusting. But today is a new day! Now that the mask has been pulled from my life, revealing the bloodline, revealing the incestuous predatorial cloth that drapes over me, and my mother. How multiple generations have been influenced, and affected by this cloth that it was supposed to protect and shield. But it was actually paper, and the edges cut inconspicuously, severing several nerves causing bleeding in my most sensitive places. Now, I have to figure out how am I going to recover from this? I can't just go to the hospital and get stitches. How do I manage all the damaged nerve endings that have now been exposed? I can't keep it covered, that only reduces the irritation temporarily, it doesn't heal my pain.

Ezekiel has always encouraged me to pray, Dwayne tried to give me a word from the Lord, and Lee is always telling me I should come to church with him and the kids - but I've never listened to any of them. Maybe God is real. Maybe he has been trying to get me prepared for this very moment. But, because I refused to listen, here I am. My Uncle Ray told me all the answers I needed were in that box. He was right. Now I am broken at the core of my very existence, and I don't know what to do, or how to get up from this pit of hell. What do I do now that I've opened Pandora's box? As the old saying says the truth will set you free...I have the truth, I see my truth...now I have to walk in my freedom, no matter how bad it hurts.

Chastity climbs in the bed facing Lee and says "Can we talk?" Lee puts down his book and replies, "Sure, what's on your mind?" She nervously says, "I have never shared my past with anyone. I have only shared snippets with you about Cheyenne, Ezekiel, and Dwayne. Tonight, I want to go deeper, I want to talk about my childhood. I opened my

Momma's box today." She sets the box on the bed, opens it, and pulls out the pictures. "Look, she and I look like twins, right?" Lee takes the pictures and responds, "Yes, almost identical. If it wasn't for hers in black and white and yours in color I would think you two were the same person." Chastity starts to cry. She then pulls out her Birth Certificate, hands it to Lee and says, "We literally are! We have the same Daddy, and the same thing he did to her, he did to me."

Lee reached over and hugs Chastity saying, "I'm so sorry baby, this was not your fault. Now I understand, and I apologize for being so hard on you. This is a lot for you to carry around all this time." Chastity tries to speak and Lee says, "Shh, you don't have to say anything, you did nothing wrong, you did what you thought was normal, what you were taught to do. You are safe now. I'm here. I'm not going anywhere, and we are going to be fine. The past is over, in God all things are made new, surrender all your pain to Him, everything you've done give to Him. He throws it in the sea of forgiveness, never holding it against you. He loves you. I love you. He forgives you, and I forgive you." Lee held her all night, and Chastity slept peacefully in his arms.

Dear Diary,

Lee is the best husband, I came to Lee broken, confused, and truly at a loss of how to move forward. He responded with love, and compassion. Lee and I sat and engaged in an honest heart-to-heart conversation about what I discovered in the box. He did not judge me, attack me, or make me feel less than because of my past. In his true mysterious way, he responded with open arms, loving arms, apologizing to me for all the things that everyone else did to me that hurt me. I could not stop the tears from flowing as he embraced me. He spoke to me with a sincerity that spoke to the inner me, and it stirred something inside of me that I never felt before. I felt safe for the first time in my entire life. He held me close, yet gentle. I felt a sense of peace. I cried until the well inside of me was completely empty, and Lee and I was fast asleep.

Every day I see a real king rising up in Lee. He is stronger and stronger, in his presence and presentation; yet he is still a mystery to me. From day to day I never know what to expect from him, he's such a puzzle - he keeps me on my toes. I believe that's the very thing I love about him. I can't control what I don't know. I really don't want to be in control, but I try to control everything. In my mind if I'm in control, then it lessens the chance of me getting hurt. I opened the chamber because I wanted to hurt others for the hurt that I was feeling deep down inside. No matter how many times I lashed out, physically on others, it never filled that empty pain inside of me permanently. It was a temporary fix to the symptom of a much more cancerous erosion.

All these years I have been trying to make the men in my life pay for the hurt I suffered at the hands of another man, and myself. Yes, I include myself in this because I was punishing myself for what Mr. Ron did to me. I never allowed myself the opportunity to fully open up to love, embrace true intimacy, honesty, and all the things relationships are meant to be. Here comes the reserve well of tears. But, I got it now, and I'm giving me, the real me, a chance to experience the new me.

THE FREEDOM WALK

Dear Diary,

I knew this conversation would be a difficult one to have because it revealed things about me I had been trying to escape for years. I always equated it to my nick name, but it was the very essence of my character. I've come to realize that it doesn't matter what name I am called, if the inside is the same, I will always be a repeat offender, it's just a matter of time before the old characteristics rise up and act up. They only shut up for so long.

I must say, finding that out helped me to figure out who and where I really was, and formulate a viable plan to get to who and where I want to be. It's a process, and a risk. No risk, no reward - I'm worth it! I'm taking my freedom!

"Good Morning my beautiful Queen." Lee says as he kisses Chastity and wakes her from her sleep. "Today is our first joint counseling session, do you still want to go?" Chastity stretches, smiles, and says, "Yes my

King, I wouldn't miss it. I'm taking my freedom." They arrive at the session on time and the counselor says, "Come on in, there are some refreshments on the table, help yourselves. How are you two doing today?" Chastity and Lee respond together, "We're good." As the they hold hands and smile. The counselor asks, "Did y'all have sex this morning?" They respond together again, "No." Lee says, "No, but we have been communicating more. We have been having more intimate conversations that have helped bring us closer, and a deeper level of trust." "I see. Please, can you share more?" the counselor asks. Chastity says, "Well, for the first time in my life, I opened up about my childhood. Lee did not judge me, he embraced me, he understood me, and he made me feel protected. I've always felt that if I escaped my nick name, Chass and had everyone call me Chastity it would change my past. I thought moving 1700 miles away would change my past. I even worked double time to break the generational curse of poverty, molestation, and education thinking that would change my past. But it didn't, it was still there haunting me all the time no matter where I was, who I was trying to masquerade as, or what name I was being called. The content of my character was still there and the predatory behaviors were imbedded in my DNA. That's not figurative, that's literal…I'm not sure how to move forward and fully recover. But, now that the mask is off I am ready to figure it out. I believe with your help, and the support of my husband I will be free to be the real me, whoever that is." The counselor claps and rubs her hands together and says, "Alright then, let's get started."

Dear Diary,

Today was a great day! Counseling was eye opening, and I now have a starting place to my freedom.

She gave me an assignment. I have to get a mask - on the outside write on it everything that I wanted people to see, and what other people say that they see, and on the inside what I really saw. So, on our way home, we stopped by the craft store and picked a few masks. Lee said he's going to do it too.

Lee also shared that he felt something break over his life when he left his job and launched his own firm. I told him, I see a difference in him, and I am falling deeper in love with him every day. I also shared with him that I am not sure if Ezekiel or Dwayne is Zion's father. He said he thought about that, and he knows at some point Dwayne will get out of prison and will come and demand to find out. He said he's glad that I owned it so we can face it together, unity destroys the enemy. I know he has me covered, that alone feels like freedom. That's the best way to explain it.

Dear Diary,

When I woke up this morning Lee and the kids had all gone to church, as usual. For the first time, I saw my bathroom and how beautiful it is. I stood in the shower enjoying the water beating on my back, as I stared at the grey veins in the granite, and the gold shadows. Although the grey is darker and dominant, the gold shadow still has prominence, and shines through boldly. It cannot be hidden, it has its own journey.

I dried myself off, got dressed, and went to the place I never imagined myself going…
church.

When I arrived, service had already started. As I proceeded from my car, I could hear the choir singing, "Oh Lord I need you to help me, Oh Lord, I need you to help me, help me on my journey, help me on my way, Oh Lord, I need you to help me." By the time I reached the door, tears were rolling down my face. I opened the door, and went inside. I could feel something on the inside drawing me into the service. I opened the next set of doors, and the usher waved her hand for me to follow her. She stopped about midway, and extended her arm to where I could sit; but, I kept walking past her, - I felt something calling me to the altar. It felt like the closer I got, the better I felt. The youth were dancing at the altar with colorful flags and ribbons, their every move was in sync with the words the choir sang, "Oh Lord I need you to help me" began to belt from the inner most part of me as if I knew the song. My hands were lifted up, and my eyes full of tears. As I approached the altar, the dancers fluidly moved out of my way without missing a step, and they continued to dance on each side of me. Two women followed behind me, and as I kneeled down at the altar, I felt their hands on me, and I could hear the wails of women crying, and praying. I was crying out "Lord I need you to help me, I need to be free. Lord I need you to help me!" I was weeping, and the women were weeping with me, and praying for me.

The last time I visited a church, I was a child. The mothers sat on the front row of the church so they could pray with the girls on the altar, now, the Deacons and Ministers have taken over that row. I don't know who these women were, but there were there with me, fighting with me, and interceding for me. I felt a light shining down on me, and I heard a still voice speak to me, "You're free, and I will change your name."

I'm not exactly sure how long I was on the altar, the next thing I knew the women were helping me up, we all embraced, and I felt as if all my pain was erased and replaced with peace. They ushered me to the front pew, and they stayed with me the rest of the service. I felt light. I felt refreshed. I felt cleansed. I felt FREE! After service was over, one of the women introduced herself to me and said, "I'm Sister Johnson, and today you got your breakthrough, there is no turning back. God has something special in store for you." She placed a piece of paper in my hand and said, "Please call me, let's stay connected. You are welcome to call anytime, if I'm not up, I will get up, and if I'm not available, I will get back to you?" I said, "Yes Ma'am, I will."

Lee and the children came and hugged me, the kids were asking if I was okay. I told them, "Yes, Mommy is excellent."

Dear Diary,

My eyes have been opened with such clarity, and I feel different on the inside. All this time I thought I could change my name, but now I realize - I don't have the power, only God can do it. It's not really about changing my name, it's about changing my heart, and my mind. So, when I say my name, it has a new meaning to me.

Now that I am establishing a relationship with God, I now see life through a new lens. Bad things aren't always happening to me, sometimes my decisions invite bad things into my path. I am learning how to walk with God, and now I talk with Him daily about everything that I do. I want to pursue life being in His will, not my own. I am finding that my freedom is through my relationship with Him. I no longer have to look over my shoulder wondering when someone will show up and expose me. I know who I was, and who I am, and the process between the two has given me God confidence, and freedom.

Dear Diary,

Counseling was very focused today. We brought our masks, discussed our view from the inside and outside of the mask. It was very eye opening. Our next steps are to forgive ourselves and others. It doesn't do us any good placing blame - it just builds more hurt, anger, and resentment. In order to be free, we have to let things go. This is not about other people, this is about the space unforgiveness is taking up in our minds and hearts. She said we could forgive them anyway we choose. We can tell the person and run the risk of them further rejecting us, or injecting more hurt on us. Or we can write it out on paper or index cards and then rip them up. As we rip them up we express our forgiveness for what they did and say we no longer harbor or hold onto any ill will toward them. Lee and I agreed that we would also say, forgive them Father for the did not know what they were doing. He showed me in the Bible - Matthew 6:14-15, that we are to forgive other people when they sin against us, so that our heavenly Father will also forgive us. Because if you do not forgive others, He will not forgive our sins. Lord knows I want to be forgiven, so I'm forgiving everybody. Freedom sure feels good, God good!

Dear Diary,

Last night I had a weird dream. I saw Ezekiel dressed in a beautiful white and gold robe. He had a beautiful gold crown on his head, and it had jewels all around it. He was sitting in this huge mansion, on a throne with a golden staff in his hand like a king on his throne. They carried me on a sedan chair, by four guards. They sat me down near Ezekiel, and I was enthralled with his majesty that I did not see Lee there until Ezekiel spoke of him. He said, "This man has presented himself here today as your husband, and asked that I release you to be his, freely. Do you want to be his freely?" I looked over at Lee and there was a part of me that wanted to say yes, but a part that is still tied to Ezekiel, and desired to say no. Ezekiel then said that I must decide, either take my life and be with him, or live and go with Lee. Just then I woke up, and sat straight up in the bed. I could barely catch my breath. I looked over and Lee was not in the bed with me. I looked at the clock and it was 1:04 AM. I got out of bed and began looking for him, but didn't see him anywhere. I finally found him fast asleep in the family room, with the TV watching him. I woke him up, and told him to come to bed. I snuggled in his chest and went back to sleep. Ezekiel came to me again, this time he was calling me Chass, and he never called me that. This time I responded with a strength I never knew I had, I said, "My name is Chastity, and I choose Lee." Ezekiel smiled and said, "It is well love."

I called Sister Johnson the next morning and told her about the dream, and she said that sometimes the devil tries to use the ones we love, those that are near and dear to us to try to destroy us. She reminded me that I had strength because I got Jesus. She was really excited that I called her. She seems like a really sweet lady, and I feel blessed to have her in my life. Now that I have been going to church every Sunday with Lee and the kids, I have been learning a lot about God, and myself. My name is Chastity, my nick name is Chass, and I am a child of a king named Jesus. With Him   I   have   freedom!

I SHALL RECOVER

Dear Diary,

I bless God that I am still walking with Him and my therapist. Today, I discovered that my need for control is because I always felt I had no control. Things were going on around me, decisions were being made for me, and I either was too young to have a say or felt powerless to say anything. I felt because of my mother's addiction, there would be no recourse for what Mr. Ron did to me. I felt like she knew, but that she too felt powerless to do anything about it. This feeling of powerlessness was projected onto me because he was her father, and the same thing had happened to her in her youth. As children we never want to hurt our parents, even when they are hurting us. When we are children we suffer in silence. We are screaming on the inside for help, yet we are lack of sound, void of words, and pressured by shame to shut up.

Shame is really the devil's child. It systematically shuts you down mentally. It strips away your self-esteem, value, and worth. It disconnects your thought process so you're unable to overcome negative thinking, and ties you to your wounds with no rope. It causes you to believe that if you say something people are going to talk about you negatively. That people won't believe you. It replays what happened to you over and over again, keeping the wound fresh, open, and painful. From the bondage of that pain rises a desire to mutilate others, for temporary relief of the internal crippling wound. There is no resolve for the agony that returns as you relive the moment of penetrating pain that persists day in and day out. In reality we never fully progress into adulthood, we are still the powerless child with no voice for what we really need. The voice we now have is a misplaced reaction to what was done to us, toward those who have done nothing to us.

As I learn more about God, who He is, and who I am in Him I realize that I am not what happened to me. It is not still happening to me. Jesus went to the cross one time, and He gave up His life one time for all my pain, shame, guilt, grief, sickness, sins and more. Where His life ends, mine begins. I shall recover it all! That's an illusion straight from the father of lies replaying my hurts over and over again in my head. Reality is, I can make different decisions. I am in a different place mentally, and physically. I have the power to embrace this moment in reality. I live where I am, not where I was. I'm living my freedom.

Dear Diary,

Today was another eye-opening day of therapy. Dominance is power and influence over another. There is positive and negative power and influence. My past was full of negative power and influence. That reality has stuck with me into adulthood. Although I was presenting a positive look, the truth is everything underneath the garments was negative. *My positives were my beautiful home, nice car, name brand clothes, and successful career. In reality it was a disguise. It was a mask over everything I was trying to hide and run from — my negatives. A house is a house - large or small, good neighborhood or bad. It's still a house, how you care for the house determines how it will take care of you. When something breaks - we have to fix it. If we put a band-aid on it - it's still not fixed. I had been placing band-aids on a lot of wounds, this is why they have not healed. My therapists asked me, "How do wounds become scars?" This is a powerful question. One that I never thought about. When I have a wound, I care for it. I clean it, put Neosporin on it, change the bandage often, check on its progress to healing daily. When I thought about this, I realized, I never do this in any other area of my life, only for physical wounds. Why? I also realized that Lee is also there to help care from my wounds, change the bandages, and check on the healing process. We are here for each other. We are help meets, not help defeats.*

Lord I thank you for changing my mind. Now that my thoughts are different, I am able to see healing different, and in real time. This feels so good to me. I have the power to heal me in Jesus name. Dominating and mutilating others doesn't heal me. Taking care of me, heals me. Taking care of my husband heals us, heals our marriage, and seals us in unity that no man can tear apart. We are wearing our freedom.

Dear Diary,

I'm enjoying the unraveling of the innermost parts of us. God is revealing to us that I am not what happened to me and Lee is not who I and his boss was making him think he was. We are finding that what happened to us doesn't define or confine us, and this has been a real breakthrough for us collectively and individually.

I now can see and walk in my purpose. I spoke at a Women's Shelter last night and it has forever changed my life. There are women out there just like me. It really blessed my heart to share with them that self-care is the process needed for healing and recovery. We spend so much time giving the perpetrator in our lives the power, that we negate our own power. Our true power, not the power we lorded over others as we became perpetrators. But the power of God within us, the power He gives us to do something different, the power to heal, be free, and recover from all that has happened. We laughed, we cried, and seven women gave their life to Christ. It was overwhelmingly good and I believe God was well pleased.

THE NEW BEGINNING

Dear Diary

Today is a day of new beginnings because today, I got Baptized! I also shared my testimony with the church. I was so nervous, but Jesus took the wheel and I was able to read what I had written.

"Today represents my new beginning. All my life, I always hid from my problems. One day, with the encouragement of my husband Lee, I decided to face them. Little did I know that it would lead me to a relationship with Jesus Christ. You see, for years I put on my "face," and lived a masquerade to the world. Behind the mask my true character was - Carnivorous, Hunting, Atrocious, Schematic, and Satanic. I thought that if I changed my name, where I lived, my economic status, got educated, and got married, I would escape my past and become this new person. But because I was full of impurities, the change I was seeking never came. It was only after my encounter with God on this altar, the day he spoke to me did I realized only He was the only one that could change me. But, I had to give him permission to do it. Today, I thank God for picking me up, and cleaning me up from the inside out. He

changed my mind — and now I think differently. He changed my heart - and now I love differently, and He wrote my name, he didn't change it — he wrote it in the book of life. He changed how I hear my name, how I say my name, and how I hear my name. Now, when I hear my name I feel free. Free to be who HE has created me to be, and He did it just for me."

The church erupted in praise and I was overcome with emotion. I am still full...

After church, Chastity came home and went straight to her bedroom. She wrote in her diary then she began to talk to God, and express her gratitude to Him. "Lord I thank you for being with me always - in all ways, for having my back, and protecting me when I couldn't protect myself. As I bare my naked body and soul to you today..." She began to take her clothes off. She was totally naked on her knees crying, praying, and experiencing God in a way that she had never experienced Him before. "God, I feel you moving right here in my bedroom, and I just want to thank you. You did it just for me, I am free, my mind is free. There is freedom in your presence, in this relationship that I have with you. You have opened my eyes and everything looks new. I no longer see disdain, and feel hate toward people, toward myself. I now see love and feel compassion for them. I love myself for the first time. Lord I thank you, you did it just for me." Chastity lays on the floor, looking up at the ceiling, with her hands on her chest. Lee comes in, and places a sheet over her likes he's part of the Catcher's Ministry at church. Chastity pulls it off, and continues to enjoy God, and begins to sing softly, "I give you all of me, I give you all of me." Then Lee puts on the William McDowell CD, "I surrender all to you, everything I give to you, withholding nothing, withholding nothing..." Lee undresses and is standing over Chastity. He bends down, and lays on the floor beside her, and he begins to pray.

"Father God in the name of Jesus,

We honor you, and thank you.

 You are our creator, our redeemer

Forgive us of our sins,

forgive others who have sinned against us,

those who have hurt us in ways we were not able to articulate.

Today we come to you, withholding nothing,

nothing hiding us from you like Adam and Eve when you first created them in the Garden, before they sinned.

We commit this day to you, we are fully surrender to you Lord,

withholding nothing from you

because you said in your word that you

draw near those, who draw near you.

We draw near to you right now, in the name of Jesus

Heal our hearts, Lord

Mend our broken pieces

Bring us together in our marriage Lord,

where you desire for us to be

Bring us to you and to each other.

The way you designed for us to be

withholding nothing, open, honest, and true

Today, we recommit, and surrender to each other

To love each other unconditionally, to be faithful to one another,

to always be there for each other, in riches, and in drought

In sickness, and in health

Until death on this earth tears us apart

Help us Lord to never fall away you or each other

We need you. In Jesus name we pray, Amen"

Lee embraced Chastity and sealed their vow and prayer in the most intimate way.

Dear Diary,

I have to come back again and tell you for the first time in 42 years, I made love to a man. I felt the love of a man. Today, I experienced what true marital sexual intimacy is, and it was with my husband Lee, my true King, and he brought me to deep chocolate!

Dear Diary

I thought Ezekiel was my king, but now I know without a shadow of a doubt what a real king looks like, tastes like, feels like. He protects, covers, loves, strengthens, provides, and brings out the best in you. A Queen helps a man see the value in his freedom, and kingship. She helps him to be better without making him feel like he owes her for what she has done. She helps him achieve all that he aspires to do, while stroking his ego and not shredding it to pieces. She makes him look good, feel good, because he treasures the value in her.

I am embracing all that God has for me and Lee. Life has been kind, and full of the riches God promised. Every day I am reminded of his goodness and I thank Him. I'm still a work in progress, and I see progress everyday as I work toward my full recovery.

I'm embracing my new beginning, for I know that victory is mine!

Ding Dong. Ding Dong. "Hello" Consuela says as she opens the door. "Hello, is Chastity here?" The older lady says with a younger gentleman with her that looks oddly familiar to her. "One moment please." Consuela says as she closes the door and nervously runs into the kitchen. "Mr. and Mrs. He's here! He's at the door! He's with an older lady…" she exclaims and points toward the front door. "Who is he? Who is here?" Chastity asks. Lee gets up and heads toward the front door and opens it, "Good Morning, Ms. Johnson, what brings you here?" The younger gentleman with her turns around and says, "Is Chastity here?" "Who are you?" Lee asks. Ms. Johnson interjects, "May we come in? Let's not do this outside where the neighbors can hear." Lee extends his arm and invites them in. "Please have a seat in here." Lee directs them to the Livingroom. The gentleman remains standing. Ms. Johnson takes a seat on the couch and says, "This is my son, Dwayne, he just came home yesterday and insisted on seeing Chastity today. I tried to talk him out of it, but here we are. Lee, I'm not sure if you know or not." "Yes, I do, I know everything. We were expecting him. We knew this day was coming." Lee responds calmly. "Give me a moment, let me get my wife. We are prepared to move forward on this matter." Lee goes upstairs where Chastity is getting dressed and says, "Babe,   it's   time.   Dwayne   is   here.

ABOUT THE AUTHOR

Pastor M. Queeni Green, affectionately known as "Pastor Queeni" brings a unique voice to the Christian Fiction genre. She identifies our deepest struggles, and trauma, and removes the clinical parameters. She provides a life applicable view to see it and deal with it.

Pastor Queeni's life experiences has shaped her bold, candid, and creative writing style. She draws the reader in through riveting story lines that have more highs and lows, twists, and turns than a roller coaster.

Pastor Queeni's Freedom Journals are an excellent accompaniment to her books as they give the reader an opportunity to look at their own lives, own their truth, and journal through it and find hope, peace, and restoration. She teaches extensively from her books in prisons, Bible Studies, Book Clubs, Conferences, and more.

Pastor Queeni's quote for life is Reach, Embrace, and Enjoy - Reach for what God is calling you to do, Embrace every opportunity to serve, and Enjoy every blessing for your obedience.

CONTACT THE AUTHOR

Queeni Sings Ministries
P.O. Box 2
Browns Mills, NJ 08015

www.queenisings.com
Info@queenisings.com

www.ingramcontent.com/pod-product-compliance
Lightning Source LLC
Chambersburg PA
CBHW072015170626

46813CB00005B/2152